NEVER AGAIN

(A May Moore Suspense Thriller—Book Six)

BLAKE PIERCE

Blake Pierce

Blake Pierce is the USA Today bestselling author of the RILEY PAGE mystery series, which includes seventeen books. Blake Pierce is also the author of the MACKENZIE WHITE mystery series, comprising fourteen books; of the AVERY BLACK mystery series, comprising six books; of the KERI LOCKE mystery series, comprising five books; of the MAKING OF RILEY PAIGE mystery series, comprising six books; of the KATE WISE mystery series, comprising seven books; of the CHLOE FINE psychological suspense mystery, comprising six books; of the JESSE HUNT psychological suspense thriller series, comprising twenty-four books; of the AU PAIR psychological suspense thriller series, comprising three books; of the ZOE PRIME mystery series, comprising six books; of the ADELE SHARP mystery series, comprising sixteen books, of the EUROPEAN VOYAGE cozy mystery series, comprising four books; of the new LAURA FROST FBI suspense thriller, comprising nine books (and counting); of the new ELLA DARK FBI suspense thriller, comprising eleven books (and counting); of the A YEAR IN EUROPE cozy mystery series, comprising nine books, of the AVA GOLD mystery series, comprising six books (and counting); of the RACHEL GIFT mystery series, comprising six books (and counting); of the VALERIE LAW mystery series, comprising nine books (and counting); of the PAIGE KING mystery series, comprising six books (and counting); of the MAY MOORE mystery series, comprising six books (and counting); of the CORA SHIELDS mystery series, comprising three books (and counting); and of the NICKY LYONS mystery series, comprising three books (and counting).

An avid reader and lifelong fan of the mystery and thriller genres, Blake loves to hear from you, so please feel free to visit www.blakepierceauthor.com to learn more and stay in touch.

BOOKS BY BLAKE PIERCE

NICKY LYONS MYSTERY SERIES
ALL MINE (Book #1)
ALL HIS (Book #2)
ALL HE SEES (Book #3)

CORA SHIELDS MYSTERY SERIES
UNDONE (Book #1)
UNWANTED (Book #2)
UNHINGED (Book #3)

MAY MOORE SUSPENSE THRILLER
NEVER RUN (Book #1)
NEVER TELL (Book #2)
NEVER LIVE (Book #3)
NEVER HIDE (Book #4)
NEVER FORGIVE (Book #5)
NEVER AGAIN (Book #6)

PAIGE KING MYSTERY SERIES
THE GIRL HE PINED (Book #1)
THE GIRL HE CHOSE (Book #2)
THE GIRL HE TOOK (Book #3)
THE GIRL HE WISHED (Book #4)
THE GIRL HE CROWNED (Book #5)
THE GIRL HE WATCHED (Book #6)

VALERIE LAW MYSTERY SERIES
NO MERCY (Book #1)
NO PITY (Book #2)
NO FEAR (Book #3)
NO SLEEP (Book #4)
NO QUARTER (Book #5)
NO CHANCE (Book #6)
NO REFUGE (Book #7)
NO GRACE (Book #8)
NO ESCAPE (Book #9)

RACHEL GIFT MYSTERY SERIES
HER LAST WISH (Book #1)
HER LAST CHANCE (Book #2)
HER LAST HOPE (Book #3)
HER LAST FEAR (Book #4)
HER LAST CHOICE (Book #5)
HER LAST BREATH (Book #6)
HER LAST MISTAKE (Book #7)
HER LAST DESIRE (Book #8)

AVA GOLD MYSTERY SERIES
CITY OF PREY (Book #1)
CITY OF FEAR (Book #2)
CITY OF BONES (Book #3)
CITY OF GHOSTS (Book #4)
CITY OF DEATH (Book #5)
CITY OF VICE (Book #6)

A YEAR IN EUROPE
A MURDER IN PARIS (Book #1)
DEATH IN FLORENCE (Book #2)
VENGEANCE IN VIENNA (Book #3)
A FATALITY IN SPAIN (Book #4)

ELLA DARK FBI SUSPENSE THRILLER
GIRL, ALONE (Book #1)
GIRL, TAKEN (Book #2)
GIRL, HUNTED (Book #3)
GIRL, SILENCED (Book #4)
GIRL, VANISHED (Book 5)
GIRL ERASED (Book #6)
GIRL, FORSAKEN (Book #7)
GIRL, TRAPPED (Book #8)
GIRL, EXPENDABLE (Book #9)
GIRL, ESCAPED (Book #10)
GIRL, HIS (Book #11)

LAURA FROST FBI SUSPENSE THRILLER
ALREADY GONE (Book #1)
ALREADY SEEN (Book #2)

ALREADY TRAPPED (Book #3)
ALREADY MISSING (Book #4)
ALREADY DEAD (Book #5)
ALREADY TAKEN (Book #6)
ALREADY CHOSEN (Book #7)
ALREADY LOST (Book #8)
ALREADY HIS (Book #9)

EUROPEAN VOYAGE COZY MYSTERY SERIES
MURDER (AND BAKLAVA) (Book #1)
DEATH (AND APPLE STRUDEL) (Book #2)
CRIME (AND LAGER) (Book #3)
MISFORTUNE (AND GOUDA) (Book #4)
CALAMITY (AND A DANISH) (Book #5)
MAYHEM (AND HERRING) (Book #6)

ADELE SHARP MYSTERY SERIES
LEFT TO DIE (Book #1)
LEFT TO RUN (Book #2)
LEFT TO HIDE (Book #3)
LEFT TO KILL (Book #4)
LEFT TO MURDER (Book #5)
LEFT TO ENVY (Book #6)
LEFT TO LAPSE (Book #7)
LEFT TO VANISH (Book #8)
LEFT TO HUNT (Book #9)
LEFT TO FEAR (Book #10)
LEFT TO PREY (Book #11)
LEFT TO LURE (Book #12)
LEFT TO CRAVE (Book #13)
LEFT TO LOATHE (Book #14)
LEFT TO HARM (Book #15)
LEFT TO RUIN (Book #16)

THE AU PAIR SERIES
ALMOST GONE (Book#1)
ALMOST LOST (Book #2)
ALMOST DEAD (Book #3)

ZOE PRIME MYSTERY SERIES
FACE OF DEATH (Book#1)

FACE OF MURDER (Book #2)
FACE OF FEAR (Book #3)
FACE OF MADNESS (Book #4)
FACE OF FURY (Book #5)
FACE OF DARKNESS (Book #6)

A JESSIE HUNT PSYCHOLOGICAL SUSPENSE SERIES
THE PERFECT WIFE (Book #1)
THE PERFECT BLOCK (Book #2)
THE PERFECT HOUSE (Book #3)
THE PERFECT SMILE (Book #4)
THE PERFECT LIE (Book #5)
THE PERFECT LOOK (Book #6)
THE PERFECT AFFAIR (Book #7)
THE PERFECT ALIBI (Book #8)
THE PERFECT NEIGHBOR (Book #9)
THE PERFECT DISGUISE (Book #10)
THE PERFECT SECRET (Book #11)
THE PERFECT FAÇADE (Book #12)
THE PERFECT IMPRESSION (Book #13)
THE PERFECT DECEIT (Book #14)
THE PERFECT MISTRESS (Book #15)
THE PERFECT IMAGE (Book #16)
THE PERFECT VEIL (Book #17)
THE PERFECT INDISCRETION (Book #18)
THE PERFECT RUMOR (Book #19)
THE PERFECT COUPLE (Book #20)
THE PERFECT MURDER (Book #21)
THE PERFECT HUSBAND (Book #22)
THE PERFECT SCANDAL (Book #23)
THE PERFECT MASK (Book #24)

CHLOE FINE PSYCHOLOGICAL SUSPENSE SERIES
NEXT DOOR (Book #1)
A NEIGHBOR'S LIE (Book #2)
CUL DE SAC (Book #3)
SILENT NEIGHBOR (Book #4)
HOMECOMING (Book #5)
TINTED WINDOWS (Book #6)

KATE WISE MYSTERY SERIES
IF SHE KNEW (Book #1)
IF SHE SAW (Book #2)
IF SHE RAN (Book #3)
IF SHE HID (Book #4)
IF SHE FLED (Book #5)
IF SHE FEARED (Book #6)
IF SHE HEARD (Book #7)

THE MAKING OF RILEY PAIGE SERIES
WATCHING (Book #1)
WAITING (Book #2)
LURING (Book #3)
TAKING (Book #4)
STALKING (Book #5)
KILLING (Book #6)

RILEY PAIGE MYSTERY SERIES
ONCE GONE (Book #1)
ONCE TAKEN (Book #2)
ONCE CRAVED (Book #3)
ONCE LURED (Book #4)
ONCE HUNTED (Book #5)
ONCE PINED (Book #6)
ONCE FORSAKEN (Book #7)
ONCE COLD (Book #8)
ONCE STALKED (Book #9)
ONCE LOST (Book #10)
ONCE BURIED (Book #11)
ONCE BOUND (Book #12)
ONCE TRAPPED (Book #13)
ONCE DORMANT (Book #14)
ONCE SHUNNED (Book #15)
ONCE MISSED (Book #16)
ONCE CHOSEN (Book #17)

MACKENZIE WHITE MYSTERY SERIES
BEFORE HE KILLS (Book #1)
BEFORE HE SEES (Book #2)
BEFORE HE COVETS (Book #3)
BEFORE HE TAKES (Book #4)

BEFORE HE NEEDS (Book #5)
BEFORE HE FEELS (Book #6)
BEFORE HE SINS (Book #7)
BEFORE HE HUNTS (Book #8)
BEFORE HE PREYS (Book #9)
BEFORE HE LONGS (Book #10)
BEFORE HE LAPSES (Book #11)
BEFORE HE ENVIES (Book #12)
BEFORE HE STALKS (Book #13)
BEFORE HE HARMS (Book #14)

AVERY BLACK MYSTERY SERIES
CAUSE TO KILL (Book #1)
CAUSE TO RUN (Book #2)
CAUSE TO HIDE (Book #3)
CAUSE TO FEAR (Book #4)
CAUSE TO SAVE (Book #5)
CAUSE TO DREAD (Book #6)

KERI LOCKE MYSTERY SERIES
A TRACE OF DEATH (Book #1)
A TRACE OF MURDER (Book #2)
A TRACE OF VICE (Book #3)
A TRACE OF CRIME (Book #4)
A TRACE OF HOPE (Book #5)

PROLOGUE

"Come on, Indiana." K-9 officer Rolf Coombes clapped his hands as the golden Labrador sprang out of the police truck, tail wagging. A dog with a high work ethic and energy level, Indiana was looking forward to his task, even though most people would find it gory at best, blood-chilling at worst.

Rolf fastened the dog's leash onto the harness, and walked over to the small group of people that stood on the grassy hill a few yards from the road.

On this bright, late summer day, the peaceful environment with the views of Indian Lake nearby and the forest across the fields, seemed at odds with the purpose of their mission, Rolf thought. This small town of Lakeside surely was one of the most scenic places in Tamarack County.

It seemed a pity that they were here for such a serious, in fact, heartbreaking job. They were here to try and track down any trace of a missing person, a twenty-two-year-old woman from Lakeside, Lily Gregory, who'd been gone for more than two weeks.

And now, after all other scenarios had been explored, her family had to face the grim possibility that she'd been the victim of foul play.

Rolf walked over to join the group of other people, which included two police officers from Lakeside, two volunteer civilians from the same community, and Mr. Gregory, the father of the missing woman.

"Thank you for coming out here." Rolf thought Mr. Gregory looked pale and stressed, as if he hadn't slept nearly enough in the past two weeks.

"I hope we can provide some answers, sir. I'm Officer Coombes and this is Indiana."

He wasn't going to give the cadaver dog's nickname, Indiana Bones. Not in front of the father of the missing woman. It would be insensitive.

Sometimes, you needed gallows humor to get through the hard job of identifying victims by having these highly trained dogs sniff out human remains in the area.

The Labrador sat obediently, tail wagging cheerfully. Indiana Bones loved to work, and lived to get results. Even if results meant finding old bones, dumped bodies, and the hint of rotting or decomposed flesh in the area, so subtle or deeply buried as to be invisible to the human nose.

"Lily Gregory was definitely seen getting off a bus on the corner of Creek Road." The police officer pointed to the road, where Rolf could see a couple of vehicles driving through the summer haze. "But she never made it home. We've searched the town, the woods. We even searched the old barns in the area. But no trace of Lily. What we've done so far hasn't worked."

"Understood, sir," Rolf said.

"So, now, we're wondering - was she murdered? And if so, could she have been dumped somewhere nearby?" the officer asked.

Rolf nodded solemnly, seeing how Mr. Gregory paled at the thought, making a visible effort to hold himself together.

"Indiana is one of our best and most hardworking dogs," he said. "We're going to search the wider area and see if he picks up anything. We'll let you know the results as soon as we can, but it might take a while." He fixed his eyes on the father's face, wanting him to know that he would do whatever it took to find answers for him.

The stressed looking man nodded. "Thank you."

"Okay, Indiana, let's go." Rolf turned and walked up the grassy slope, toward the trees.

Once there, he turned to the dog, unfastened the leash, and gave the command to search. The Labrador bounded off the grass and started to run, his long tail wagging enthusiastically.

Rolf knew that this was likely to take a while. The area between the bus stop and the farm where the Gregory family lived, which was demarcated on the map he had with him, spanned a couple of miles. The lake bordered the dirt road, and there were a couple of trails that cut through the nearby forest and on through the fields beyond.

It always seemed somehow dissonant to Rolf when he was asked to search such an idyllic area. But he knew that it was in these remote locations that bodies were dumped. Although he and Indiana did their fair share of work in old warehouses, in drains and construction sites and abandoned buildings, the truth of it was that when most people wanted to hide a body, they drove out of town.

He knew that Indiana was a thorough dog, who would cast around an area, picking up the scent, and would then check carefully before being ready to move on to the next. This dog would not miss a detail.

But, to his surprise, this time when he let Indiana go, the dog barely hesitated. Purposeful and focused, he set off at a run, veering away from the woods.

Concerned by this unusual behavior, Rolf jogged after him, watching as Indiana made his way unerringly along the narrow, winding path that led through a grassy field and into a low-lying meadow, one that Rolf had noticed from the road, because it was a riot of color.

The green meadow, with long, un-mowed grass, was filled with summer flowers, blooming in their pinks, whites, reds, and yellows.

He stopped abruptly, staring in surprise as Indiana Bones gave the signal that he had sniffed out remains.

The dog sat down and barked once.

Human remains? There? So close to the road? And picked up so fast?

The dog was trained to know the difference between human and animal corpses and never once had he made a mistake. But even so, Rolf felt surprised as he ran down to join him.

A body - dumped or buried in the meadow?

As he approached and looked more closely in the corner of the meadow, Rolf saw the ground looked churned up. The grass and flowers were growing over humps and bumps in the soil, but concealed among the blossoms, he saw traces of raw earth that made his spine prickle at what it signified. So this was a shallow grave, for sure, but more importantly, a recent one.

He felt a pang of apprehension. Just a couple of miles from the Gregory farmhouse, and clearly so freshly buried, it could well be that Indiana Bones had discovered their daughter's murder.

And then, to his astonishment, Indiana Bones stood up. He walked a few paces, nose to the ground.

Then he sat and barked again.

Rolf's eyes narrowed in astonishment. A second body? His dog was well trained to sniff out multiple corpses, but he'd never had the opportunity to put this particular skillset into practice before.

Had this killer used the site as a dumping ground previously?

Perplexed, he approached, and then his eyes widened as the dog did the same again. He moved a few more paces, this time to an area where the grass and flowers grew thickly, and there he stopped, sat, and barked once more.

"You sure, boy?" Rolf asked in a soft, disbelieving voice.

Arriving at the scene, now perspiring with anxiety, Rolf took in the details as the dog signaled yet again. The earth below was well hidden by the overgrowth of grass, the riot of summer flowers. But all the same, it was giving a perfect, clear message to his brave cadaver dog.

Without a doubt, this meadow was home, not just to one murder victim, but to a mass grave. Numerous bodies must have been buried here, and from the state of the ground, at different times, because there was only one patch that looked to have been recently dug up.

With the sweet smell of grasses and flowers on the breeze, Rolf found his stomach churning with dread.

They were on the verge of discovering something big here. He feared it would be something worse than anything he'd yet seen in his ten-year police career, and his five-year career as a K-9 handler.

Something terrible, that had been hidden away for months or years in the peaceful field in this quiet community.

The ground that had been hiding these atrocities was about to reveal its secrets. This unmarked and secret grave site must surely have been used again and again.

He didn't want to speak the words 'serial killer' aloud. Not yet, not until he was sure, not until the people who were qualified to assess such a catastrophe had arrived to excavate this site.

Because Rolf, with a chilling certainty, knew that Lily Gregory was probably going to be the last victim placed among the multiple corpses who lay here.

But she was not going to be the first.

CHAPTER ONE

Deputy May Moore stood at the counter in the locksmith's store, biting her lip anxiously, hoping that this time, on her third try, she would get answers to the problem that was consuming her mind.

It was a worn, wooden counter, and the store itself was tiny and hot. Morning sun streamed through the window and she saw dust motes dancing in it. The air smelled of oil and metal.

But May was all but unaware of her surroundings, because her focus was on the two keys on the counter.

They were clearly a pair of keys. Similar looking, of the same age and type of steel, but one was longer than the other.

These keys had to be related to the disappearance of her sister Lauren, ten years ago. May felt sure of it.

The shorter one had been found in the evidence box from her sister's missing person case. She'd unearthed it when she'd reopened Lauren's case a few weeks ago. It hadn't been listed anywhere in the contents. Its presence was a mystery.

And then, the mystery had taken another strange turn when May had been left a threatening video, anonymously warning her to back off and stop digging into this old case.

She'd been shocked that the grainy footage showed Lauren, storming out of their parents' house on the day she'd disappeared. Someone had been watching her and filming her on that day. And this same someone was now threatening May.

Scared, but needing to know more about who was sending these threats, May had searched around and found where the video must have been taken, in an old, abandoned churchyard a couple of blocks away. And she'd found the second key there, in a pile of gravel. It must have been dropped, right where the person who'd taken the video had been standing.

That had been two weeks ago.

Whenever she'd had time, May was now trying to find out how these two keys were related, and what they could possibly open.

Her search had led her to two different locksmiths who hadn't been able to figure it out more specifically beyond stating that they were probably safe keys. But the second one had recommended someone local, a specialist who might know more about safes in the area, and given May his address.

Now, on a Saturday morning, she had finally found the time to visit him. Pete's Locks was in Chestnut Hill, and from the look of the shop, Pete had been doing business in this same place for decades.

Pushing back her sandy blonde hair, May regarded the slim, gray-haired man anxiously as he stared down at the keys, turning them, peering at them, feeling their edges and the steel shafts.

"Interesting," Pete murmured to himself.

She watched as he picked up a magnifying glass, leaned over the counter and studied the two ends. Then he frowned and looked up at her.

"These keys are from an older type of safe," he said.

"An older safe?" May asked. She felt encouraged. Finally, there were answers.

"These open an old dual lock safe. One where both the keys have to be used simultaneously to gain entry."

"Are they common, these safes?"

He raised a graying eyebrow as he stared at her through piercing blue eyes.

"No. Not so common, especially the ones that require this length of key. I'm going to photograph them, if you don't mind. I've worked on a few of these safes in my time, and I can try to go through my records and see if we can narrow the options down."

"You mean, you might actually be able to figure out where it comes from?"

"If it's from the area, there's a possibility," he said. "Don't bank on it. But there were only a few of these particular safes here, to my knowledge. They were big and expensive, and very often, one or other of the keys would get lost, because of the dual locking system. So we worked on a lot of those that were here. Let me have a while to think. Perhaps we can find answers."

He looked at her, his face kindly.

May felt a flash of gratitude that in these puzzling and strange circumstances, she might just be able to get a clearer answer. At any rate, this man, with his expert knowledge of the area, represented her best chance.

"Thank you," she said. "I really appreciate it. It's very important to me to know."

"I can see it is," he said sympathetically.

At that moment, May's phone beeped. Instinctively, even though it was a Saturday, she glanced down at it, needing to know if it was anything important, if she should drop what she was doing and rush into work.

But it was her older sister Kerry texting her.

Curious, May read the message thinking that, on a Saturday, it would probably be something about the wedding. More than likely, a favor she wanted May to do, one of those 'quick favors' that would end up taking the entire day. But when she opened the message, she frowned. This was not a favor at all.

"May, there has been a disaster! Can we speak?"

May peered down at the message, wishing she could read her sister's mind, because 'disaster' was a relative term. In the build-up to her sister's highly anticipated wedding, it seemed that every day presented a new crisis that simply had to be attended to immediately.

She didn't want to say that top-achieving FBI agent Kerry was becoming a Bridezilla. But it sure was feeling that way after the entire family had been drawn into preparations for the wedding, which would take place in their hometown of Fairshore.

May could immediately isolate two possibilities that might have triggered this 'disaster' message. The first was that the woman who was hand-designing the custom invitations hadn't come up with a pleasing enough design.

And the second was that, after May had called around and sourced ten different menus from local caterers last weekend, her sister didn't like any of the options so far.

She didn't feel ready to discuss either one with Kerry at this moment. Not when she was standing with somebody who might, literally, hold the key to Lauren's disappearance. That took priority over invitations and caterers.

So she texted, *"I can't. I'm busy researching Lauren's case."*

Kerry replied almost immediately. *"Oh."*

May frowned at the message, which was so brief and restrained it almost hurt. What kind of emergency was this, anyway? May didn't want to raise this question with Kerry. She knew she would find out if it was important. A moment later, her phone beeped again.

It was another message from Kerry.

"Okay, then. I need to talk urgently. It's a crisis! Call me as soon as you're done."

"Will do," May texted back.

Staring at the keys again, she forced her mind away from potential wedding disasters, and back to the burningly important issue she'd arrived here for.

"How long do you think it will take? To get answers, I mean?" she asked the locksmith.

"If I have time, I'll work on it this weekend," he said. "I enjoy a puzzle. It keeps the mind active. And as I said, I can see this means a lot to you."

"It does. It's a family matter," May emphasized. And just to be honest with this kindly man, she added, "It's a personal issue of my own. It's not related to an active case, just so you understand."

"I'll try my best, no matter what it is. Of course, it all depends on who comes in for help, or gets locked out of their own house accidentally." He smiled wryly. "But I'll be in touch as soon as I can, Deputy Moore."

He glanced down again at the business card she'd given him.

"Thank you," May said. It was time to go. She didn't want to take up any more of this kind man's time.

As May walked outside, her phone started ringing. She almost didn't answer, sure that it would be Kerry, all out of patience and needing to speak immediately.

But her number one rule as the county's deputy was always to check her phone, as she never knew who might be needing her and for what. And sure enough, this time, it was her boss, Sheriff Jack, on the line.

Quickly, May picked up.

"May. Sorry to have to call on a weekend." Her boss sounded tense and stressed. Immediately, May knew there had been a crisis. Her heart sped up.

"What is it, Jack?" she asked.

"We have a very serious situation. A cadaver dog has just sniffed out a mass grave, in a meadow outside of Chestnut Hill. So far, more than ten bodies have been discovered. The most recent one is only a couple of weeks old."

May drew in a gasp of horror. She knew immediately which body Sheriff Jack was referring to. This must be Lily Gregory, who had gone missing about two and a half weeks ago. May had been told by the Chestnut Hill police that the cadaver dog would be on site today to search for any remains in the area.

But a mass grave? That was an absolute bombshell. It didn't seem possible that such a thing could exist in Tamarack County. How long had it been there? Who was buried there? Questions surged in her mind.

"I'm on my way," she said. "Please send the coordinates. I'll get there as soon as I can."

Thrills of unease coursed through her as she wondered how on earth a missing person case, involving one potential victim, had escalated so fast. What was going on?

She ran for her car. As she got there, her phone buzzed with the incoming coordinates.

Glancing at them, May accelerated away, heading for this creepy mass grave at top speed.

CHAPTER TWO

May accelerated along the quiet country road to where the coordinates led her, feeling shocked and disbelief that such a catastrophe could be playing out.

In Tamarack County? Outside the calm town of Chestnut Hill, in a stretch of countryside that May had always thought was particularly beautiful.

Now, she saw the road ahead was crammed with cars. And not only cars, she realized. There were vans there, too. And a fence had been opened so that two earth moving machines could access the flower-filled meadow just a few yards from the road, which was a hive of activity.

Milling around, close to the site, were men from the police, the county, the forensic team, and the coroner's office. White-suited techs were clustering around the area. The crackle of radios filled the air.

The sight of the meadow made her feel a clench of regret, because she remembered that Lily had last been seen near here. She had gotten off the bus at the stop by the main road in the evening, before she'd vanished. The bus driver had remembered her clearly. This meadow was close by, though a few hundred yards in the other direction from Lily's parents' farm.

Clearly she had not been taken far and the killer must have been ready to pounce. He must have been watching and waiting. No way could such a crime have been coincidental, not with the number of bodies found.

This disturbing fact resonated in May's mind as she paced across the road and hurried down to the scene. She hoped that with so many personnel on site, answers could be found, because they surely needed them.

The question that she didn't even dare to think about simmered at the back of her mind: What if Lauren was among these victims? How far back in time did these graves date? She felt flooded with anxiety as she approached the scene.

There was Sheriff Jack. She saw his rangy, gray-haired figure. He was speaking to a white-coated tech wearing foot covers and a mask.

May hurried to the edge of the field, heading to him. As she did, she heard a shout from behind.

"Hey, May!"

She turned, to see that Owen Lovell, her deputy, had just arrived. There was his car, parked facing hers. He must have gotten here seconds after she had. As the tall, dark-haired man rushed down the embankment of the road to join her, May felt a surge of relief that he was on the scene.

Owen's presence always made her feel that any catastrophe was in capable hands. And more than that, she couldn't help feeling a flutter in her chest as he approached.

He'd recently escaped death after being caught in a bomb blast and basement fire. He'd only been cleared for return to work last week, after ten days of medical leave to ensure that he had no after-effects from the smoke inhalation which he'd suffered worse than she had.

That time without Owen had made May realize how much she had missed him, how much she valued the intelligent deputy who was her partner. And it made her regret, all over again, that she had not agreed to date him when he'd asked her.

She felt, deep in her bones, that it had been a wrong decision to say no, made through fear of the future. May didn't want her life ruled by fear and reluctance. She didn't want to be that kind of person who would be so terrified of change or disappointment that she pushed away the chance at love and happiness.

She was rethinking, drastically, what she'd done.

But there was no time to worry about that now. Not when they both had to go and meet their boss, so that they could learn the full extent of this shocking scene.

"May, Owen." Sheriff Jack rushed over to them. "Let me update you on what we have here."

"Please," May asked her boss, eager to know any information that might shed light on this terrible crime.

"As you know, Lily disappeared over two weeks ago. Since she was definitely seen getting off the bus, and never arrived two miles away at her home, we made a decision to intensively search the area. When there were no results, we brought in the K9 corps. And today, that ended up getting us far more than we expected." He sighed. "We are uncovering and documenting the bodies, but so far, there are eleven."

"Eleven?" Owen gasped.

May shook her head. This was hard to take in. "Are they all in the same stages of decay?" she asked.

"No. We have the most recent one, which we believe to be Lily's body, which the dog picked up first, near the edge of the area. Then, beyond, about a yard or two apart, there are others. Mostly bones. You can see that as the timeline goes back, the soil is less disturbed and has had a chance to settle, but these are shallow graves. Only a couple of feet deep."

"Has the coroner examined the most recent one already?" May asked, thinking uneasily about Lauren again. She forced herself to remain calm and pushed the worries about her sister out of her mind. Only time would tell, and in any case, she was here to serve the community. Every victim deserved her full attention and focus.

"He is making a start with it on site, so that if it is Lily, we can notify her parents immediately. He's working in the trench we've dug, and will do some preliminary work there as the others are unearthed."

Jack paused, shaking his head, clearly distressed by what he was seeing. "Go over and view the site. You will have valuable input, I'm sure. At the moment there are obviously two main priorities: to identify who all these victims are, and to find out who did this."

Finding out who did it was a huge priority, May knew, because the last kill had been so recent. This murderer was still active. Even now, he or she could be tracking down another victim.

"Will the FBI be involved?" she asked, thinking immediately of Kerry.

"Yes, I've just notified them. They are putting a team together, including some forensic experts, and they'll probably be arriving tomorrow morning."

May turned to look at the site, briefly wondering if Kerry would form part of that team. She probably would, May decided, and if so, she'd better make sure to call her back this morning, or Kerry would be mad at her by the time she arrived.

But for now, calling her sister was way down on the list of priorities.

She paced over to the area that resembled a cross between a crime scene and an earthworks. With the bodies uncovered, her nose could pick up a hint of rot, but it was underscored by the fresh smell of damp, rich soil. She could even pick up the scent of flowers, May realized. Was there a hint of jasmine and rose in the air?

It was bearable at least to stand here, and for that she was grateful. But as county deputy, she needed to do more than just observe. She needed to give her input and ideas that could hopefully lead to an early breakthrough in this brand new murder case. And she also needed to get down and dirty, and give hands-on support where it was needed. Even if right now, that literally meant getting into the trenches.

"Morning, May," the coroner called, looking up and seeing her there.

She knew the local coroner, Andy Baker, well.

"Morning, Andy," she said. "This is such a shock. What are you busy with first?"

"We're organizing all the bones to be analyzed. I'm working on the most recent body to see if there's any evidence we can pick up. So far it seems certain that it is Lily Gregory as there's a bracelet that matches up with the one she was wearing. The bodies all seem to have been clothed when buried, and to have some possessions with them. We're finding a few items already."

"Such as?"

"Purses. Jewelry. So we should end up with a fair amount of evidence."

These possessions on site indicated that this killer had not murdered the women for what they had. Jewelry and money had not been his motive. But she would have been surprised if it had been. More likely, they were killed for who they were, what he perceived they had done to him, or what they meant to him. Those were some of the motivations, May knew, for why serial killers did their grisly work.

May looked at the scene. The bodies were surprisingly close together, some almost jumbled up against each other. She guessed that working blind, with no markers in place, the killer had simply guessed where the old burials were, when digging his new shallow graves.

In that case, May wondered if he could have made a mistake and mishandled something.

"Let's get all the bones fingerprinted," she said. "Perhaps he might have ended up moving one or more of them, or touched them, when burying a new body."

Andy raised his eyebrows. "Good idea. I'll ask them to do that," he said. "We'll send everything straight for fingerprints. We're getting that done as a rush job, just to see if there is anything obvious. The full forensic exam will take a lot longer."

"That sounds like the best plan," May said. She was happy with the prints being prioritized.

Already, the fingerprint techs were beginning to work their way methodically around the scene, dusting each group of bones and items as they went.

May decided it was time to be truly hands on here.

She went over to the equipment box, and pulled on a coat, foot coverings, a head cover, and gloves. The protective equipment felt sweltering on this warm summer day, but she knew the discomfort would be more than worth it if this killer could be found through trace evidence on site.

She didn't want to do this. But she needed to know who these victims were and help get this scene processed as speedily as possible.

She'd never done anything like this before. She felt scared and unsure that she would not be good enough, or that it would be too much for her to handle.

Then May shook her head. She had to draw on all the inner strength she could, just as the other brave people on scene were doing. And she was sure that there must be clues hidden down there, things she could pick up, evidence that could be important and make a difference, even if it was only in a subliminal way at this point.

"I'll help you down there," May said.

Taking a deep breath and gathering all her courage, she jumped down into the trench, and walked over to the first pile of bones, ready to see what secrets it might reveal.

CHAPTER THREE

Dressed in her PPE, May was already sweltering in her plastic and latex. But she knew that it was all-important not to contaminate the scene. In this shockingly unexpected dumping ground, it was likely that there could be secrets to the killer's identity.

After all it was already clear that he had visited this scene time and time again.

It chilled May to think of how a person could have done that.

"What can I do?" she asked Andy through her mask.

"Here, May. I'm searching through the initial dumping grounds. I'm noting anything that gives us an immediate lead. These bodies have been dumped carelessly. There are items of clothing, purses, possessions. You can photograph and note anything helpful on site, and record these belongings before they are placed in a body bag with the victims' remains," Andy decided.

"I'll do that," May said.

"Here we have something," Andy told her. "A purse. It's in good condition. Take a look through, see if you can find anything helpful."

May took the purse in her gloved hands. Carefully, she opened the faux leather, which was covered in soil. But there was a driver's license card inside. She photographed it, seeing with a thump of her heart that it belonged to Laurel Denford. She remembered Laurel's missing person case, which had been active two years ago. Two years!

She'd lived all the way in the north of Tamarack County, in a remote small town. After her disappearance, there had been a massive hunt for her. Her two brothers had kept it up, with posters and patrols, for months. Eventually the consensus had been that she must have drowned while hiking near one of the area's lakes or rivers.

May felt unbelievably sad to be staring down at this muddied, disintegrating possession which told her otherwise. Her family would finally have closure, but in such sad circumstances, May was sure it would provide more questions than answers.

She knew that a lot of heartbroken families were now going to be asking these same questions, and that she and her team would need to provide answers - as well as a guarantee that this killer could not continue to wreak this destruction and murder.

Again, her thoughts flitted briefly back to Lauren as she placed the purse carefully in an evidence bag and handed it back to Andy. Could he have taken her? Would her body be found in the next few hours, nothing more than a sad, dry pile of bones?

Taking a deep, shaky breath and trying her best to banish the awful possibility from her mind, she carried on with the hard and messy work that Andy was handing to her.

Already, a chain of processing this evidence was in progress. May saw the first van pull away, containing four body bags. It would be taking the remains to the pathologist's office, where everything would be checked for any fingerprints before further tests and analysis were done. Owen was also heading there, she saw, driving determinedly behind the van. She felt glad about that, knowing that her partner would be assisting with the fingerprinting to get it done as fast as possible.

But in the meantime, her job was here.

She moved carefully along the outside of the excavation site, where Andy handed her a wallet. The leather was dirty, but otherwise in a reasonably good state and May guessed this might be one of the more recent remains, though she was trying her best not to look. It was all she could do to stand here; it was taking all of her courage.

Working so closely with remains was way outside of her comfort zone.

The wallet belonged to a woman called Daisy-Mae Ridgeway. May caught her breath. Everyone had thought Daisy-Mae had been a runaway after her boyfriend had broken up with her. She'd been twenty-two years old when she had disappeared a few months ago, but with one parent dead and the other estranged from her, the search had not been as intensive, and although her case was still open, it had been shelved in the likelihood that she'd left town of her own accord.

Now, May was realizing differently with a sense of doom.

She photographed the evidence carefully.

On the surface, all around the scene, the police and other teams were going about their business. May knew that they were all doing their best to get a grip on a situation which was spiraling out of control.

But, as far as she could tell, no one was making any headway yet.

These were the innocent people he'd scouted out without anyone seeing or noticing his actions, who he'd been watching, who he'd taken, who he'd killed, although she had no idea how. The most recent victim might provide the clearest answer as to how he had committed his kills.

She was sickened by the idea of how many times he must have killed here, in this county, enjoying the thrill of watching his victims, and planning his crimes.

As she handled the possessions - a frayed necklace, a pair of movie tickets that had somehow survived inside an inner pocket, a chain store credit card with another victim's name clearly displayed, and even a cellphone, its screen blank and dead - May began to feel as if there was no end in sight.

Faced with this amount of destruction, she could not help but have the uneasy conviction that the killer had already won. She knew there was so much they didn't know. There was so much that they would need to find out to have any chance of catching this killer. This felt like the worst nightmare that a deputy could imagine.

May lost all track of time as she focused on the task at hand, deliberately walling off her emotions. She worked steadily, mechanically, with Andy handing her the items, and May photographing and noting each one. She took a break to drink some water, but then jumped straight back down into the excavation area, which she now saw was beginning to take the shape of a rough circle.

Her phone beeped again and she glanced down at it, hoping it might be Owen, messaging her with some news on the fingerprints.

May grimaced as she saw it was Kerry again.

"Hey, sis! You done with work? This is really urgent. I mean, it's a catastrophe!"

Shaking her head, May put her phone away. She genuinely didn't have time to speak to Kerry now. Not while handling a catastrophe of far greater proportions right here, close to her hometown of Fairshore.

May felt a tremor of fear.

This was so much bigger than she had ever imagined. The list of victim's names which was being drawn up by the team working hard on a laptop computer in the police van by the site, was getting longer and longer, the dates of their disappearances stretching back years.

Already, May knew it was going to be one of the largest serial murder investigations in the county's history. And that's saying something, she thought, grimly.

He had been at this for a long time, and there seemed to be no end in sight. Who could he be? How could he possibly have done this and not been caught? Was he taunting them, hating them so much that he wanted to show them that he was smarter than they were?

May could not help but feel a shudder of fear and despair. This was becoming so much of a nightmare, but she had no intention of quitting, even though every time Andy moved on to a new victim, May felt unsure again whether she could cope. She was wet with sweat under the PPE. She felt as if she'd been down in this grime and earth for hours. But May reminded herself that the victims had been there far longer, with nobody to help or protect them from their fate.

She told herself firmly that she was not going to give up on this.

She was not going to let this man win.

So, making sure that she moved with energy and purpose, she accompanied Andy for a final check around the site, to see if anything had been dropped on the perimeter.

And then, her phone started ringing.

Thinking it would be Kerry, but hoping it wouldn't, she quickly pulled it out of her pocket, her sweaty fingers slithering in the gloves.

It was Owen. Quickly, she swiped the answer button.

"Hey, May? Are you able to come through to the police department?" her deputy asked, sounding excited.

"Sure, I can come through now if it's urgent. What's up?" May said, glancing at Andy who nodded.

"We can get someone else in here if you have to go," he muttered.

"I'm here at the coroner's office. We've identified a fingerprint," Owen said. "We have a clear print on one of the bones, and I've been able to get into the local database already. I'm searching for a match now."

May felt a thrill of excitement. This was exactly what she'd hoped for, that in coming back again and again to his dumping ground, the killer had finally grown careless. And a match? If that could be found, it meant a firm lead from someone whose prints were on record.

"I'm on my way, right now," she said.

CHAPTER FOUR

May rushed into the county coroner's office, feeling enthused about this strong lead. A fingerprint was real, solid evidence. Having it tracked to its owner so early in this terrible case might at least ensure that a swift arrest was made.

She was feeling a good few degrees cooler than she had in the blazing sun on site. Once in the car, she'd stripped off her PPE and put on a fresh blouse, having rushed to site in the pink T-shirt she'd worn for her Saturday morning trip to the locksmith.

Now, she was wearing the blue, collared shirt she always kept in the trunk of her car for work emergencies.

She nodded a greeting to the attendant at the front desk.

"Morning, Deputy," the woman greeted her. "Your team is in the lab on the right, but your partner is in the office at the back."

"Thanks," May said.

A bustle of activity in one of the laboratories on the right, told her that the fingerprinting was still under way. The teams were not stopping until they had checked all the bones. She could hear Sheriff Jack's voice in there, calmly directing this operation.

May ran straight through to the back office where Owen was waiting.

He had his laptop out, and had accessed the fingerprint database. As soon as she walked in, he turned to her, looking enthused.

"I'm so impressed I got access to this immediately," he said. "There wasn't even a wait. It must be because it's a weekend. And it's just come up with a match! Look at this, May."

"Who's it for?"

"It's for a man called Petrus Baker. I see his fingerprints are on record because he was a suspect in a robbery case a few years ago, but charges were dropped due to lack of evidence."

"Hmmm," May said thoughtfully, leaning closer. "And what work does he do?"

"I'm looking now." Owen gasped as the database he needed flickered into view. "Well, can you believe it?"

"What?" May crowded closer.

"He's a cemetery manager!"

Shivers cascaded down May's spine. This was most definitely a strange, and creepy, potential link that needed to be explored.

Had Petrus Baker developed an obsession with the dead, killing victims and stocking up his own private graveyard in a remote site?

She took a look at his ID photo. It showed her a grim-faced man who looked to be in his forties. Petrus Baker had a shock of dark hair, and eyes that stared coldly at the camera.

A cemetery manager. She couldn't believe it.

"He manages the local graveyard site in Chestnut Hill. May, I think we need to speak to him immediately," Owen said.

"We can be there in ten minutes, if we drive fast. Let's take my car."

Picking up the purse she'd put down on the desk, May hustled for the door.

*

Ten minutes later, she accelerated up to the cemetery entrance.

May seldom came inside here, but she drove past it frequently and had always thought that this medium sized graveyard was a well-kept place. Never before had she wondered about the mindset of the man in charge, but now she was wondering if they had missed something, and if somehow, he should have come to her attention before this time.

They were one of just four cars in the well swept public parking area. May's mind was racing as she and Owen jumped out of her car and headed to the graveyard's main entrance.

It was now early afternoon, and clouds were gathering, blotting out the sun with their dark shadows.

She felt unable to get rid of the image in her mind of this graveyard manager, arriving to bury a new body, digging in the wrong place, and shoving a bone back under the soil before moving to a fresh location.

What would they find when they confronted this man? And where would he be?

May saw that there was a central office building not too far from the gate. The modest building seemed to consist of a small lobby and a larger back room.

"Could he be in there, perhaps? Or maybe they know where he is?"

May walked in and came face to face with a woman in a cleaner's uniform, who was busy polishing the desk.

"Good afternoon," she said. "We're looking for Petrus Baker. Is he here, do you know?"

The woman shook her head. "It's Mr. Baker's day off today."

"I see," May said, disappointed. She'd forgotten that while they were hard at work, it was actually a Saturday, when many of the working world took a weekend.

May was so used to working weekends in her career as a policewoman that she barely noticed them anymore. Especially since there was inevitably a surge in violent crimes, DUIs, and other offenses on Friday and Saturday nights, which spilled over into Sundays.

She guessed they would have to find out where he lived. But then, the cleaner spoke again.

"If you need him, he's probably at the church down the road. He tends their graveyard, one Saturday afternoon each month. You'll most likely find him there."

"Thank you," May said. Undoubtedly, this cemented the fact this man had an obsession with graves. And now, they knew where he would be.

The church down the road was visible from the graveyard parking lot, and was only about four hundred yards away. May and Owen climbed into the car again and set off, feeling glad of this new lead that had allowed them to pinpoint their suspect when he was still close by.

"What is it with this man and graves?" Owen asked in a low voice as they set off down the road.

"I don't know. But it makes it even more important that we question him as soon as we can," May agreed.

When May climbed out of the car at the churchyard a minute later, she sensed immediately that it felt like a very different place from the official town cemetery.

This was an old church, and the grave site was no longer used, and clearly had the bare minimum of maintenance, just to stop it from becoming an overgrown wild land. It was a sprawling place, with graves interspersed between looming spruce trees. One side of the site had a high stone wall; the other framed the graveyard with a dark, overgrown hedge.

With the sun now buried by clouds, it felt like even more of a threatening place.

At first glance, May could see there was far too much work to be done for one afternoon a month to cope with it. That was probably why the site looked so untidy. And the overhanging trees made it surprisingly dark. Gazing around as she walked, May almost tripped over a stony outcrop, all but hidden behind a tuft of grass.

"Let's find this Mr. Baker, and ask him a few questions," May muttered, her voice sounding tense.

A twig snapped in the distance, and both of them jumped. But it was just an overhead branch, breaking off in the wind that was now gusting.

"We need to find him quickly," Owen whispered.

"Shhh," May said. "I hear something."

They both stood still, and listened. There was a sound of distant digging. The metallic sound of a shovel being slammed into the earth.

May and Owen paced toward the sound, which was coming from behind a huge marble gravestone, well over six feet high and wide, surrounded by spruce saplings. But as they approached, their footsteps crunching over the stones and gravel, the digging suddenly paused.

A resounding silence followed, broken only by the gusting of wind, ever stronger, through the wild, low tree branches.

And then, they stopped dead as they heard a man's voice, speaking in a growl, loud and clear. May shuddered as she heard the snarled words, filled with a vicious intent.

"I can see you. Don't think I can't see you both, sneaking up on me like that. One more step in my direction, and you'll both feel the edge of my shovel. I promise you that. It'll break your bones. And then, I'll toss you into one of the graves."

CHAPTER FIVE

May stared at Owen, appalled. This man, this cemetery manager, was off the rails. Psychotic. And even now, he must be crouched in his hiding place behind the tombstone, ready to lash out at them with his shovel.

"I'm going to try and grab him," Owen breathed. "I'll go around this side." He pointed to the left of the large marble slab.

"Okay," May mouthed back. "In that case, I'll go that way." She pointed right.

With their plan in mind, they began sneaking around in each direction.

May knew that they would have to move fast. They had no idea what they would find when they rounded the corner and came into a confrontation with this man.

He must have had a vantage point through the trees that was invisible from their side, because she couldn't see him at all from her side. She had no idea where he was or whether he was facing left or right as he uttered his snarled, gruesome threats. Did he even know they were police?

May considered shouting out that they were police, but she didn't think it would help. After all, if her blue collared shirt and Owen's Fairshore Police Department jacket, and both their hats, had not already told him they were law enforcement, then he clearly knew but didn't care.

Together, in step, she and Owen paced quietly in their separate directions. May felt her heart pounding in her throat as she reached the edge of the tombstone. Out of the corner of her eye, she could see Owen readying himself.

At exactly the same time, they both leaped forward.

May had no idea what they would see or which way their attacker would be facing. She was ready to jump on him in an instant if he was faced toward Owen. She didn't want her partner to get hurt!

They both rounded the corner at the same time.

"Hands in the air!" Owen yelled.

But to May's astonishment, the cemetery manager was not looking in either of their directions. He had his back to the tombstone, and was staring ahead of him at a point in the trees.

May thought she saw a sudden flurry of activity from that point, as if a large, furry rodent, or maybe more than one, had scuttled for cover.

And then she had no time for anything, because with a startled cry, Baker swung in Owen's direction, brandishing his shovel, looking panicked at his sudden appearance, which May now wondered if he maybe hadn't been expecting at all.

He didn't even look as if he was seeing them clearly or understanding who they were. He looked like a man trying desperately to defend himself from a sudden and surprise attack.

May grabbed for the shovel's handle, desperate to stop the man from swinging it in Owen's direction. But she was too late. He was already launching it, crying out as he wielded the heavy metal shaft with its hard edge.

Owen dodged the swinging shovel, but stumbled over a tree root and went sprawling down.

Now snarling in fear, Baker raised it again. "You're not going to get me!" he shouted.

Owen jerked to the right as the shovel came down with a thud. May grabbed for his arm again, but to her consternation Baker yanked it free, showing surprising strength.

Now, forgetting Owen, he turned on her. May felt fear flare as she saw his muscles bunch, and that heavy shovel swing back over his head again.

What was this man doing? Was he even in his right mind?

May had to try and talk him down from what she realized was a panicked mindset where he was not thinking clearly at all. After all, the situation couldn't get worse. He was already thrashing at them with a heavy shovel that, if the blow hit, could do serious damage or even kill.

"No!" May cried out. "Don't do it! We're police! Police! We're not here to hurt you. Put the spade down!"

Baker paused, the shovel raised above his head. She thought she saw a flash of confusion in his eyes.

And then, from behind, Owen managed to struggle to his feet and grab the heavy metal handle, holding it back, preventing Baker from bringing it down for another attempt at a maiming blow.

"Police," he reiterated in gentle but firm tones, which May felt admiring that he was able to summon up at such a tense time. Her deputy was doing his best to contain and defuse the other man's panic.

And May now saw an expression on Baker's face she genuinely had not expected. It was a flash of utter relief.

"Police?" he echoed incredulously. Owen lifted the shovel easily from his hand. Just as well, because a moment later, a flash of doubt crossed the cemetery manager's face. "You sure?"

Quickly, May grabbed her badge from the inside of her jacket pocket and showed it to him.

"Well. You are police. So you weren't kidding." Baker sounded impressed. "So you weren't the rats I saw just now?"

"Wait, what? Rats?" May said incredulously. "Do we look like rats?"

"There were two rats in the bushes over there." He pointed. "They were looking at me strange. And I will tell you now, especially on a stormy afternoon like this, I've seen the dead take on the form of animals, and then change back. In this graveyard, there are a lot of restless spirits. That's why everyone else refuses to tend it. I'm the only man who is prepared to spend time in here, and I can tell you, some of the things I've seen and heard would chill your spine."

May had definitely not expected him to explain that. But it did make sense, based on how scared he'd been, and the scurrying noise she had heard as they had rounded the tombstone. His reaction to their presence was now understandable. But it indicated to May that he was an unstable man, prone to believing things he imagined.

Or perhaps not. She stared around her, feeling a sudden chill on her face, as if an icy gust of wind had flurried past.

Before she got too creeped out by their surroundings, May knew that they had to get to the gist of what they had arrived here for. This man was a suspect in a multiple murder case, and with good reason, since his fingerprint had been found on a bone in this mass grave. The presence or absence of ghosts and spirits at this time was a secondary issue and she couldn't allow it to distract her.

Even if she felt a strange, cold breath on the back of her neck that made her spine tingle.

"Sir, we didn't see any rodents behaving strangely," May tried to reassure him, rubbing her neck to get rid of the chilly shivers. "But we do need to ask you a few questions."

"Sure. What questions?"

"We found your fingerprint on a bone in a mass grave we've just been excavating," she said.

Baker squinted at her as if she was the one who was now raving mad.

"What are you talking about? A mass grave? Did I hear you right? What mass grave? Where?"

May stood her ground. Evasion tactics were not going to work here.

"A mass grave of murder victims. It's in the meadow of flowers just off the main road, past Chestnut Hill. About a five minute drive from here." May pointed in the direction of the site.

"And you found my print on a bone?" He shook his head, looking totally confused.

"Yes."

There was silence for a while, broken only by the shrieking of the wind. May tried to ask him again, hoping that if she prodded him, he might come up with some information.

"In the meadow near here. Do you go there ever?"

Baker frowned. And then, his face cleared and he nodded.

"If it's the meadow I'm thinking of, I walk my dog, Spike, near there. We walk all around this area, and I remember we often bypass a flowery meadow just off that main road. And something is coming back to me now. I do remember an incident there, but it was months ago. And there weren't flowers then. It was just after winter, when everywhere was a sea of mud."

He rubbed his chin thoughtfully.

"What happened?" May asked.

"It was Spike. He went digging and unearthed a bone."

"So you're saying Spike found it?" May asked.

"Yes. I vaguely do recall he came out of a muddy hole with a bone in his mouth. It gave me a scare at first. I thought it was a human bone at first, but then I realized of course it couldn't be, not there between the roads and the woods. I realized it must be a deer bone, and I was mistaken."

May waited, feeling conflicted about this explanation, as he continued.

"I do remember throwing it back in the hole and stamping it down, and telling Spike he mustn't scavenge. You see, there's always the chance someone poisoned a critter or did something nasty. A dog could suffer for that. Especially at that stage, I didn't know the area well. And I'm training Spike not to dig."

May thought about what he'd said. There was something she needed to confirm.

"You said you didn't know the area well. Why's that?"

"Because I only moved here a year and a half ago. Before that, I lived in Ohio. I moved here for the job opportunity, and because my mother wanted to come here to retire. She's always liked the idea of a rural, lakeside retreat. We vacationed here once before and liked it. So I got the job, which came with a small two-room cottage near the graveyard premises, and we made the move."

"Okay," May said.

Though a little eccentric, Baker's version was now making sense. She felt somewhat disappointed that the story of the bones did, in fact, add up. The chances of a dog digging something out of that shallow grave in mud season were strong.

And having lived in Ohio meant he would have been simply too far away to allow for these murders to have been committed. The corpses and remains they had found in that grave stretched back for years.

So he was cleared.

"Thank you," May said. "That's all we'll need from you. Take care." They turned and walked away. She felt frustrated that a lead that had felt like a certainty had gotten them nowhere, and now they would have to start afresh.

As they left the graveyard, May's phone beeped yet again. She saw it was Kerry.

"May! There is a CRISIS! This is UNPRECEDENTED. I need to speak to you! Please!! Can I call? Now? NOW??? Let me know!"

May felt a flare of worry. Even for Kerry, this was out of character. What was happening in her sister's life? Something seemed very wrong.

"I have to give Kerry a call," she said to Owen, and walked a few steps away, now feeling curious and rather worried to hear what the huge emergency was that had erupted in her sister's life.

CHAPTER SIX

The scents mingled in the hunter's world. That was how he thought of himself. A hunter. He could pick them out. All of them. The sweet smell of jasmine. The aromatic, caressing odor of lavender. The smell of rose, with its undertones of fruit and musk overlaying its floral notes.

He could smell everything in the mall right now, from the whiff of coffee coming from the kiosk to his right, to the lemon scented polish that had been used on the tiles this morning.

This mall had a distinctive smell. If he was dropped in here, blindfolded, he would know where he was.

His keen nose was both a blessing and a curse, that he knew. But his sense of smell had shaped his calling in life, it had defined what he needed to do to get a balance back. For years, in fact, decades, it had inspired him to choose the prey that he targeted. To bring back justice to his world and try to kill the monsters that haunted him.

He was a hunter.

He was tall, with a broad chest, strong arms and legs. He looked fit, athletic; even though he was now in his mid-thirties, he was as strong as he had been in his twenties, when his first prey had been taken. He felt a pride in his body, that he kept it so. He needed his strength for the moments when he had to lift and carry, dig and bury. These were moments when the hunt and the kill were visceral and physical.

There was no place for a weak body and an unreliable mind.

He did not indulge in drinking, smoking, or any drugs. In his line of work, he needed to be clearheaded, alert.

It was pure, unadulterated joy, to be able to do those things. He needed no other pleasures in life than to feel he was getting revenge on the voices and torments that had haunted him for as long as he could remember.

"You're worthless. You are ugly, useless, a shame to me. You deserve to be locked away in the dark, until it breaks you. You deserve a beating. And you're going to get one. Now."

The words resonated in his memory, lacerating his soul with their poison.

Pushing the chilling thoughts away, he returned his mind to his mission. He was ready to close in and stalk a new prey, carefully chosen.

He had dressed in unobtrusive colors. Taupe pants, a brown shirt, beige shoes. Colors that would not attract the eye or draw attention. His hair was neat.

He was incognito. He was invisible. And he was going to take his next victim. He'd identified her earlier, and this had been easy to do. He knew everything about her. Research was part of his mission.

Her name was Rosemary Pharr.

She was slender and tall, and today, she wore a black, knee-length skirt, and a sleeveless white blouse. Her black hair hung past her shoulders in a straight sheet.

She had a weekend job in the mall, which was to walk around and hand out perfume samples that attracted people to go into the department store and make a purchase. The hunter liked that, because it fit well with his mindset and needs.

She was good at her job. He could see that. She approached people in a friendly way, with a smile. He had watched her through the afternoon. And he saw that she was capable of putting on a show; she was quite a convincing saleslady.

Nobody was turning down her offer. She had an attractive smile. Her teeth were white and even.

He felt a moment of envy. That natural friendliness, that ability to communicate, was a skill that he did not have. He was not good at small talk. It was a skillset he sorely lacked. But luckily he seldom needed it.

But he had chosen to be alone now, and he did not regret his choice or the price he'd paid. He didn't need to talk to get what he wanted, as long as his targets were the women he chose.

Stalk, not talk.

His lips curved in amusement as he considered the words that described his actions and mindset. Stalk, not talk.

He had made the right decision for his own personality. There was no need for speech, most times. He worked mostly in silence. His language was generally the smells and fragrances that he picked up in the air.

Flowers, perfumes, and especially that smell he would always remember, one that reminded him of cruelty and pain, but which now carried the promise of death and revenge. His hand dropped to his pocket, where he kept the bottle he needed. His liquid gold, as he thought of it. The scarce treasure that he needed to complete the cycle of his revenge.

He watched as Rosemary walked down the mall, stopping every few steps to offer a sample to a passerby.

He was careful to stand behind her, and to approach from the side. And he did so, stealthily, without any sudden movements. He was long practiced in this. He knew how to move with the shadows and disappear.

He didn't seek glory or recognition in what he did. He would never brag about his skills. He just had a calling, a need. This is what he was meant to do. And being alone had freed him to be his true self, without the need to worry about anyone else's needs or expectations.

He did one thing, only. He chose to do what he craved, and that was all. He did not wish for any accolades, or for anyone to slap him on the back. That was not how he was wired.

And he did not wish to be in the spotlight. He was a shadow. In the darkness was where he belonged. It was fitting enough, since he'd spent so many painful and terrifying days locked away in the blackest dark.

As he walked behind Rosemary, he kept his eyes lowered. He didn't want any of the people milling around to see him. He didn't want to be noticed, and usually avoided eye contact with everyone.

Taking a deep breath, he inhaled the smells of the mall, the perfumes coming through the air, wafting and swirling around him, as if he were a cork bobbing in the sea, carried along on the wave of the scents.

He was alert, aware. If he'd been blindfolded, he could still have followed her through the mall, just by picking up that tiny cloud of fragrance from her samples. But he didn't want to be blindfolded. Thinking of that brought back a thrill of fear, of old memories that were hidden deep in his mind.

He reached down and took out the perfume bottle he kept in his pocket, the special, scarce one. Inhaling it now would ready his mind and prepare him for what he needed to do.

As he breathed it in, he started to tremble. It was time. This scent was telling him so.

This scent was his calling. He felt his heart beat faster at the thought of what he was about to do. He felt the thrill of anticipation, of heightened attention, almost as if he was getting ready to do a jump out of an airplane. The need he felt was sharp, as sharp as the blade of a knife.

He was a creature of ritual. These rituals would lead him to the one moment when he would take possession of his prey. That sensation of possession, that moment of ultimate excitement honed his senses to a fine point. But he was patient and didn't hurry. He knew that being cautious meant that he could work without being noticed. He would wait until her shift was over and follow her home.

"Rosemary", he murmured. He said the name softly, knowing that it was hers, even in this world of scents and smells.

It was the call to her. He had stalked her, and now he was ready to hunt her. He had his capture carefully planned, and knew exactly how he would carry it out.

She would leave this mall alive.

But she would not be alive for long. The hunter would see to that, as he followed her home.

CHAPTER SEVEN

May walked away from Owen, anxiety flaring as she dialed Kerry's number, wondering what was going on to make Kerry so frantic.

She had an uneasy feeling this was more than just a matter of the catering or the wedding cake order. Something was very wrong in her sister's life.

Kerry picked up after just one ring.

"May!" she said. Her voice sounded tense and stressed. In fact, to May's concern, she sounded almost to the point of tears.

"Kerry. What's up?" May asked, anxiety tightening. Was her sister okay?

"There's been a disaster."

"What disaster? What is it?"

"The wedding's off!" Kerry gave a sob.

Kerry, crying? That was as hard for May to take in as the bombshell she was releasing.

"The wedding's off?" she repeated in shock.

"Yes, it's off." Kerry spat out the words, with a mixture of anger and tears.

"But - but why?"

"Why do you think? Because I've broken up with that lying cheat who misrepresented himself to me so badly!" Kerry's voice exploded in her ear.

"Oh, no!" May felt shattered by this news.

She'd thought Kerry's fiancé was the perfect man. The perfect partner. He'd seemed kind, caring, adoring. Watching them together had made May feel happy, but also brought a deep sense of her own inadequacy, because how could she ever manage to find someone as perfect, who would make her as happy?

And now it seemed he was not perfect after all. He was flawed. A cheater!

May felt a thrill of fear. She literally didn't know how anyone would ever dare to cheat on Kerry. What had he been thinking? Did he not know her sister's capacity for payback?

If he didn't, May felt sure he would find out soon.

"I'm so sorry," she said, knowing the words were not enough compared to the scale of this disaster.

"I can't believe it," Kerry said, sounding almost hysterical. "I thought he was the one. I've never loved anyone like I loved him. And now he's just gone and ruined everything."

"How did you find out?" May asked, feeling sick.

"I started realizing there were inconsistencies in his stories. And he was so protective over his phone you would think it was in the Official Secrets Act. He lied and lied, and then I started pressuring him, and then I started looking into what he was doing. And he finally confessed last night. I mean, after I'd busted him red-handed, practically, in the very act," Kerry said, her voice rising in anger.

"That's - that's unbelievable!" May exclaimed.

"I mean – how can someone do that? Who does that? Why does he think that's going to work out for him?" Kerry was angry now. Her voice shook with it.

"I don't know." May didn't. She really didn't understand the actions of this man, at all. Cheating on Kerry?

"I don't know how I'm going to tell our folks. They're going to be so disappointed," she said, and now May could tell she was crying.

Again, May felt flattened by shock.

It was sounding as if Kerry was afraid of telling her parents. Afraid of seeming less than perfect. And that was so unlike her that May wondered for a moment if she'd ever truly known her older sis, or if she'd gotten so much wrong along the way.

"They'll understand," she soothed her, feeling astonished she was having to do this. "They will definitely understand and they will be as angry with him as you are. I bet Mom sends him hate mail."

Now Kerry snorted, a mix between a laugh and a sob.

"Do you want to come over here?" May asked. "I know you'll probably be called here tomorrow anyway, with this big case we've got on the go, but maybe you could come earlier? Spend the night?"

Anxiety tightened inside her as she gave the invite, because she was far, far too busy with this bombshell of a case to be able to cope with an upset Kerry. But even so, family was family and a crisis was a crisis and she had to rally.

Kerry sighed. "I got the email about the case. I haven't done more than glance at it, but I'll read through it properly. I would love to come now, but I can't." May felt a spark of relief as she continued. "I've got to finalize a few details on another case at the office tonight. If it wasn't for that, I'd be in Fairshore already. But as it is, I have to sit here, knowing what Brandon's done, looking at his things - the ones I haven't thrown over the balcony, that is. The few that we bought together that I'm keeping."

"That must be so terrible," May sympathized.

"It is but I have to keep busy. That's the only way I can deal with it, to keep busy. But I feel like I don't have enough to do."

"Are you sure you threw all his stuff over the balcony?" May suggested. "I mean, there's nothing you might have missed?"

"Trust me, I did a thorough job," Kerry snarled. "The only thing that made me feel a bit better was watching him run through the traffic this morning, trying to pick up his Calvin Klein underpants from in between all the passing cars. Then, when he got back upstairs, I locked him out and threw the ring down."

May's eyes widened as she imagined the scenario.

"He deserved it," she said bravely.

She glanced back and saw Owen looking at her in concern. As she'd paced up and down outside the church, she guessed he'd picked up enough of the conversation to get the gist of what was happening. She'd have to tell him the full story when she got off the phone with Kerry.

Little did Brandon know that this was only phase one of the payback. It was the knee-jerk response. But Kerry never stopped there. There would be a phase two, that she knew.

All Kerry's family knew what she was like when she got mad about being unfairly treated, because she'd been the same way from a young age. She put a lot of energy and imagination into making sure she got even, again and again.

But for now, to keep Kerry's mind off her misery, she wondered if her sis might possibly be interested in helping her with the project to track down the threat video.

"If you have some free time this evening, and you feel like getting your mind around a puzzle, I can send you something to look at," she said hesitantly.

"Go on?" There was a spark of interest in Kerry's voice.

"It's a video. I got home one day, a few weeks ago, and someone had put it on my laptop. They'd broken in to do it. It's warning me off searching for Lauren. That's basically what the video's about," May explained.

"And someone kept that and threatened you?" Kerry sounded incredulous.

"Yes. I don't know who it was. But it must have been someone in town at that time. I've figured out it was taken from the old mill. I found another key there, and they belong to a safe, apparently."

"The old mill. That was run as a sightseeing location for a while by a guy - what was his name? Birch? Mr. Birch?"

"I don't remember."

"It was the name of a tree, definitely. Mr. Pine? Mr. Fir? I'll have to think. I think he might have moved out of town by then, but he could be worth investigating."

As Kerry spoke, May felt a flicker of insight.

Something her sister was saying was triggering a logical connection in her current case. She could feel her mind accelerating as she drew the strands together. She thought that speaking to Kerry might have given her a lead. Her mind just needed to take the next step, and figure out what it was.

"Send the video," Kerry said. "I need to get busy with something today."

"I will, sis. And try not to be too upset. We'll talk later, okay? And there's no rush to tell the folks."

"Okay," Kerry agreed.

May hung up.

And at that moment, in a blinding flash of insight, she realized what Kerry's words had triggered in her mind.

"Owen," she said, running back to the car. "I was talking to my sister."

"Yes, I heard that," he said, sounding concerned. But now, May was too intent on following her lead to properly update him on Kerry's breakup.

"Something she said made me realize that there's a common factor in all these victims. It's such an obvious one. And it must mean something."

"What is it?" Now Owen sounded as excited as she felt.

"I'll tell you. In fact, better still, I'll show you. There might be more proof by now. Let's go back to the police department, and take a look at the list of victims. And then, you'll see what I've picked up."

CHAPTER EIGHT

The afternoon was darkening into evening as May led the way into the Fairshore Police Department. Hope fizzed inside her as she walked into the police department, intending to head straight for the back office.

She knew she had made an important connection and couldn't wait to share it with Owen.

What she didn't yet know was what it meant. But it must be a way they could use to get closer to the killer. It was a glimpse into his mind. May was sure of it.

Usually, at this hour on a Saturday, the police department was quiet. Those on duty would already be heading out, ready to police the roads and the trouble hotspots for the Saturday night partygoers.

But today, with this macabre discovery, the police department was still a hive of activity.

As soon as May walked in, she saw people waiting in the lobby. With a thud of her heart, she recognized two of the parents who'd had their children go missing, years ago. They were standing in the lobby, looking anxious, speaking together in low voices. Clearly, they were anxious to know if their missing children had been found. There were others standing there who she didn't know and she suspected a couple might even be from out of the county. She guessed the killer might have cast his net far and wide in his hunt for victims.

She could not walk past them and ignore their plight. Instead, May stopped and greeted these two parents personally, feeling a rush of sympathy for their predicament. What a terrible situation to be in, knowing that such a grave had been found, and suspecting now that your child had been one of those targeted by the killer.

"Good evening, Mrs. Pearson. Good evening, Mr. Evans," she said in a low voice.

"Deputy Moore," Mrs. Pearson replied. "Is there any news on Heather?"

"We're going to see what the latest findings are now," May said quietly. "There have been a number of graves found. We're identifying as many as possible of the victims, as fast as we can. If we get confirmation that Heather is one of them, we will be calling you personally, or else if you're still here, we'll come and tell you, because we want you to know as soon as possible. So please keep your phone open."

She included Mr. Evans as well in her request and he nodded solemnly.

Passing by the front desk, she could hear that the officer manning the lobby was on the phone to the media. From the stressed look on the junior officer's face, May guessed he'd been fielding many similar calls today.

"I'm sorry," she heard him say. "I can't give out any information at this stage as the team is still working on the case. As soon as they are ready, we'll be releasing a media statement. But for now, they have to work undisturbed on such a serious case."

Pleased that he was handling this well, May went through to the back office.

There, Sheriff Jack was coordinating the investigation, looking pale and stressed.

"May, did your lead get anywhere?" he asked immediately.

"No. The man touched the bone by accident. His dog picked it up," May said, feeling a shiver of horror that such a thing could even have happened. "He only moved here a year and a half ago from Ohio, and I see that we have older cases than that."

Jack nodded. "We have found twelve bodies, and the oldest goes back well over a decade. Almost all of them have been identified now. A few are from out of the county. It's beyond belief to think that this killer has been hiding out in our community for so long, undiscovered."

May shook her head. It simply boggled her mind to think of such evil being committed. How patiently and quietly the killer must have worked.

"We have no new leads yet," Jack said, sounding frustrated.

"I don't have a lead, but I do have an idea," May said. She hoped that her idea would take them somewhere.

"What is it?" Jack asked.

"I noticed something about the victims, and we can check if my theory is correct now that we have more names."

She paused. She hoped Jack would agree that this was worth pursuing. Because it surely was strange, what she was about to propose as an idea.

"Go on?" Now Sheriff Jack was looking curious. So was Owen, who was wide eyed with expectancy. A few others on the team were looking up from their clustered groups, spaced throughout the back room as they worked together on the different files.

"It occurred to me that all the women who have been killed - and the killer seems to have targeted women - have flowers in their names."

Jack's eyebrows shot up.

"Flowers?" he asked incredulously.

There were some murmurs of surprise from around the room.

"Yes," May said. "Obviously it's just a theory and it might be wrong, but from what I've seen so far, it was a common factor."

"We can check it," Jack said. "Let's take a look at the names we have so far." He looked down at the list. "As well as Lily Gregory, we have Daisy-Mae Ridgeway, Laurel Denford, and Heather Pearson, who's just been identified."

May felt a sinking of her heart. So Mrs. Pearson's daughter had been targeted.

"Any others?" Owen asked.

"We have just identified Jonquil Andrews, Leonie Rose, Ann Jasmine Mills, and Marigold Hayes. The final two bodies we are still working on, but I suspect one of them is Petunia Watson, who went missing fifteen years ago. All the victims are female, aged between eighteen and thirty-five. And yes, their names also provide a common thread." He stared at May, with surprise and admiration. "Most definitely, the names all have flowers in them."

Lauren's name didn't. May clung to that as the only sign of hope that her sister might not have been among those taken and targeted by this killer. Lauren had no flowers within her name. But all the others did.

Owen was nodding. "It's worth pursuing. Perhaps this killer might have been obsessed with those names. He must have known who his victims were, and picked them out for that reason. Maybe he collected information on them, and stalked them online, or followed them around. If we can find out what he found out about them, it could give us a clue about why he targeted them. And having been operational in the area for such a long time, he has to have been living locally for the past fifteen years or so."

May nodded, feeling encouraged that Owen was taking her theory further. What he was saying, and the way he was expanding on it, made sense.

"I'm going to go out and pay a personal visit to the two parents waiting outside," Sheriff Jack said. "Heather Pearson has been identified and I would like to tell her mother the news face to face. It doesn't seem like Mr. Evans's son is among the dead." He turned to May. "In the meantime, we have a starting point. We can take this further. We need to find out why there is this connection, and why the killer has been targeting women in this way."

That was their next task.

To find out who this man was. And May knew what her starting point was going to be. She wanted to speak to the parents of the very first victim. Because perhaps the killer had started out with a strong connection to Petunia Watson, and had then gone on to embark on a weird and creepily personal killing spree over the years.

CHAPTER NINE

May felt nervous as she dialed the number for Mrs. Watson. May's call would be her second phone call from the police that evening. She'd been informed already that her daughter's remains had been found.

Ideally, she would have given the grieving mother some time to process this terrible news, and perhaps paid a personal visit the next day. But there was such pressure of time on them now. They needed to act, to find out who this killer was, and to prevent more deaths from occurring.

She had her starting point. He was a man who'd been obsessed with women who had flowers in their names. He'd targeted them, hunted them down. He must have stalked them patiently before murdering them.

May hoped that Mrs. Watson would be able to accept this, as she dialed her number.

She lived far out of town, on the borders of Tamarack County, on a farm. According to the case details, twenty-year-old Petunia had been taken while walking from the bus stop to home. Very similar to the most recent victim, May realized. It seemed as if this killer liked to target his chosen kills this way, although she was sure he would have other methods up his sleeve if he needed them.

The phone rang and rang. On the fifth ring, it was picked up.

"Hello?" a woman's voice said hesitantly.

May felt a twist of worry to be speaking to a grieving parent who really should have time and privacy to process what had happened. "Mrs. Watson?" she asked.

"That's me," she replied in soft tones.

This is Deputy May Moore. I would like to give you my condolences. This must be a terrible shock. Are you okay?"

"Yes, I - I guess so," Mrs. Watson said slowly. "I am just battling to process all of this. The phone call has brought it all back. The pain, the worry. We knew Petunia was dead, that there could be no other reason why she disappeared like that. But even so, it's difficult."

"Are you able to speak to me about your daughter, and answer a few questions?"

"Sure. If it helps find this monster, I can do that."

"There seems to be a common thread, a connection, that he has been targeting women who have flowers in their names," May explained.

"Flowers? Is that so?" Mrs. Watson sounded incredulous.

"Yes, that's correct. So I wondered, were there any connections of Petunia's who were involved with flowers? Did she know anyone who was a gardener, a botanist, anything of that description? Did she work with perfumes at all?"

There was a thoughtful pause.

"She might have. I'm not sure. But I can't think of anyone who would have been close to her who was specifically interested in flowers. Her friends were mostly other people from our farming community. She did work for a fashion store, in town, on weekends. But they didn't sell perfumes; it was a clothing store."

"What about her boss? Did she ever mention him in a negative way? Or any colleagues at her workplace who might have rung alarm bells in any way?" May was determined to uncover every possible idea.

"She did say that the owner of the store, who was also the manager, was very picky and had strong opinions about how the store should be run. He was a strict man, ran a tight ship. But he passed away a couple of years ago, from a heart condition. He was about seventy-five by then, I should think. I really can't think of anyone else. She had a calm life, if I can put it that way. She was a gentle young woman."

Not the boss, and no other known contacts.

"I appreciate your help, and please let me know if you think of anything else," May said.

"I will. I hope you find this murderer, Deputy Moore," Mrs. Watson said in heartfelt tones.

May hung up, wishing that she had gotten a better lead from the first victim's mother. Fifteen years ago - at least - this man had started a campaign of terror and annihilation.

She saw that Owen was busy speaking on the phone, and guessed he was in contact with the parents of another of the earlier victims.

But from the way he was talking, and his body language, she could see that he was coming up against the same problems she had.

They were going to have to do their best to force this killer out of hiding, because for years he had been laying low in the community, unseen and undiscovered. It might have been too much of a coincidence, May now saw, if he'd been closely connected with one of the earlier victims.

But she still wasn't giving up hope, and was going to explore them all.

She looked at the list and saw that Owen had checked off Jonquil Andrews. That meant in terms of their timeline, the next earliest was nineteen-year-old Marigold Hayes, who had disappeared twelve years ago.

May picked up the phone and called the Hayes' residence, but the number just rang, so May left a message when it went through to voice mail.

She hung up, seeing that Owen had finished his call and was drawing a neat line through the name, his lips pressed together.

May was about to contact the next one on the list when Sheriff Jack rushed through again, his face drawn with worry.

"May. Owen. We have a new disaster."

May felt her stomach tense. A new disaster? She'd thought that it wasn't possible for any other catastrophes to happen on this terrible day.

"What is it?" she asked, wondering what on earth Jack was going to say, doing her best to prepare herself for what it might be.

"We've had a missing person called in. A twenty-five year old woman, who was working part-time at the local mall. She was supposed to be home two hours ago. She's not home." He paused. "Her name's Rosemary Pharr."

May felt a sense of dread. That name was like a cold slap in the face. It felt as if the killer was taunting them.

"He could have taken her," May said. "That name. It's possible she's a target."

"That's what I'm thinking," Jack said. "I've called around to all our local police departments giving them the description we've received of her, and they're going to send vehicles out, looking for her. If there's a chance we can find Rosemary, we need to take it."

"What can we do?" May asked.

"Whatever work you're doing here, let someone else carry on with it," Jack directed her. "I need you two to go to the mall and meet up with Rosemary's boyfriend, Chuck, who's there now, waiting for you."

May nodded. That was a priority now. Tracing the route Rosemary had followed, figuring out where and how she had been grabbed by this murderer.

She didn't wait for anything further. She headed out of the crowded office with Owen close behind.

They had to save Rosemary! Whatever it took, they needed to find this killer before he claimed another life.

CHAPTER TEN

May saw Chuck, Rosemary's boyfriend, as soon as she arrived at the mall. Chuck was pacing up and down outside the entrance, looking frantic. At this hour, the department store and other shops had closed, and this side of the mall was mostly empty, although there were still cars parked on the opposite side, near the movies and restaurant section.

She hurried over to the tall man with dark hair and a goatee beard.

"Deputy, thanks for coming here. I don't know what could have happened to her. I was going to come fetch her because it looked like there was a big storm threatening, but she said not to worry, it looked like the storm was going to bypass us, so she'd walk."

He glanced up at the clouds, which were still amassing in the sky, but the storm itself was moving south.

"What time would she have left?" May asked, trying to keep a calm demeanor, even though she felt helpless and panicked inside, and could see Owen frowning worriedly.

"The store she does promotions for closes at five on a Saturday. She wraps up at about quarter to five. It takes half an hour to walk to my place, where she stays."

It was now after seven-thirty. It was twilight, soon to be dark. What could they do? How could they catch up with this man in time?

"Did you try and call her?" May asked.

"Yes. Her phone was turned off. I saw that she last looked at her messages just before five, but when I tried to text her again, it didn't go through."

"I think we need to walk the route she would have taken to go home," May decided. "Let's see if we can see anything that might help us work out her movements."

"What do you think has happened?" Chuck asked anxiously as they started out from the mall. "I heard on the news that there was some big mass grave found. It sounded really creepy. Could she have been grabbed by this guy on her way home?"

"We have to accept it's a possibility," May said. "But we're going to do whatever we can to find her."

Chuck shook his head, now looking close to tears.

"She's such a sweet girl. She didn't deserve for this to happen."

While they walked, although she was scanning their surroundings carefully, May knew she needed to take the opportunity to question Chuck.

"Did Rosemary mention anything strange, anything unusual, anyone following her, in the past few days?" she asked.

Chuck shook his head. "Her job was only a weekend job. She was studying during the week, working toward her degree in marketing. Everything was, like, normal. I was also working hard. I'm a site supervisor and work shifts, so I'm often at work long hours. But I can't say there was anything that was worrying her."

"Is there anyone you can think of who might have been following her, or showing any signs of interest in her, at all? Even just a guy at the mall who was a bit too friendly?"

"No way," Chuck said, his voice indignant. "Rosemary wasn't the kind of girl to attract weirdos."

May nodded, feeling disappointed but not surprised. For sure, this killer did not make mistakes easily. Because if he had, they would not have been excavating a mass grave earlier today.

"She would have turned down this road," Chuck said, peeling off the main road that led past the mall, and walking down a smaller side road. This road was very quiet. May saw that on the right-hand side, it bordered a large park. If she'd been the killer, this was the place she would have chosen to take Rosemary.

Perhaps they would find some clue. Recent experience in her own life had proved to her that sometimes there were clues to be found. And they desperately needed to catch up with this killer, who had a lead on them and who seemed to be disturbingly invisible.

"What does Rosemary look like?" May asked.

"She's tall. She has dark hair, longer than her shoulders. She's slim," he replied.

"Do you remember what she was wearing?" May then asked.

"This morning? I wasn't home when she left, but I think she would have worn a white top and a dark skirt. That's what they liked her to wear for work at the mall."

"Your relationship has been going on for how long?"

"Six months," Chuck said. "I was thinking that we might talk about getting engaged, or maybe even married, soon. She was a lovely girl."

"You must have many happy memories," May said, trying to comfort him, and distract him from the anxiety that she knew he was feeling, and which she felt, too.

"She couldn't wait to complete her degree and get into marketing. The job at the mall, she hated it. She's allergic to perfume. Like, totally allergic. She can't wear it at all. It gives her a sinus infection and makes her sneeze. Even handing out samples was difficult for her but she did it. She was so motivated. So brave. And now she – she might be dead."

May felt sick to her stomach at these words. And then, just as she was trying to work out what else to say, Chuck stopped in his tracks. Staring at the grass to the left of the sidewalk, he gasped.

"That's her brooch," he said.

"Her brooch?" May repeated.

"Yes." Chuck was staring at it, as if hypnotized.

Following his gaze, May saw it, too.

It was a small, slender, silver pin with a pink rose on it. May guessed the rose was made from pink glass, if it was cheap, or else semi-precious stones, if it was more expensive.

She didn't have enough knowledge to tell, other than that it looked pretty. And it was distinctive. There were not likely to be many of these ornaments lying around. Without a doubt, this was Rosemary's, and the fact it was lying here was a sign.

And not a good one.

"Don't touch it!" May said instinctively, as Chuck reached down for the brooch.

He froze, and Owen quickly got an evidence bag out of his pocket. He teased the brooch into the evidence bag using the bag's edge, and without touching it.

Chuck watched, his eyes wide, as if he was only now taking in the reality of what this all meant, and the implications of this brooch lying here.

"You think - you think someone took her? That this came off her top somehow?" he asked in a shaking voice.

"It might be a sign, yes." May had to tell him the reality, difficult as it was to accept.

May looked around. The only house near this point had darkened windows, and the owners were clearly not home. Across the street, the park looked empty. It seemed like the killer had gotten lucky. Or maybe it wasn't luck. Maybe very careful planning, and a knowledge of the area.

Was that a scuff mark on the grass? She thought it might be. But it was no more than a smear, a few distressed and dented blades.

Was that a splash of blood, darkening the grass?

May thought it might be and felt a pang of consternation. Please, let her be alive. Let them be able to find her in time, she thought.

She stepped away from the area. Radioing in to headquarters, she gave them the coordinates. "Can you send a pathologist here? We've found a personal item belonging to the victim as well as a trace of what looks like blood. I'd like to get that confirmed, and tested if possible, to see if it matches up with the victim's DNA."

"We'll send a team out immediately, Deputy," the tech said. "Please wait there until they arrive."

Everything about this scene indicated a quick capture, instant unconsciousness, and then, she guessed, Rosemary must have been shoved into a car. Would he hide her somewhere? He must know the burial ground had been discovered. It might take him a while to find a new one. She wasn't going to let go of her hope that Rosemary was alive. She was going to continue searching.

Chuck was looking overwhelmed, as if this was all too much for him to handle. May didn't blame him. With a killer so prolific, she felt as if it was too much for her to handle. She had no idea how they were going to catch this evil murderer, who was preying on his victims for no other reason that the significance of their names in his warped mind.

"Thank you, Chuck," she said gently. "I'm really sorry this has happened. It's terrible and it's frightening for you. Please take care, and try to find someone to be with you tonight. The police will be in touch with you, and will probably want to take away a couple of Rosemary's personal items for DNA analysis. Just in case," she said sympathetically, not wanting to dwell on the worst case scenario, but needing to prepare him for what the police would routinely do.

"I understand," he said in a shaking voice.

"We're going to do whatever we can to find her," May said.

"We'll be in touch," Owen added.

They watched as the forlorn looking man turned and walked away. May felt as if her heart was going to break for him. And now, they had another terrible job ahead.

"I hope we find her alive. But if we don't, we'll need to look for her body. In that worst case scenario, what would he have done with it?" she asked Owen quietly.

He shook his head. "He seems to need to bury his victims in meadows. Could he have gone back to the crime scene?"

May shook her head. "No way. There will still be people there. Lights set up. Police around."

Owen frowned. "I guess that means he might look for a new one."

"We need to find out where," May said.

It was imperative now to track this killer's movements. His habits would not change, she was sure of that. But he would have had to find a new burial ground.

As soon as the forensic team arrived to manage the scene, May and Owen needed to work out where Rosemary could possibly have been taken. His gravesite had been discovered and the killer could not go back there. Terrible as it was to have to follow his gory trail, the sooner they could discover where Rosemary had been taken, then the better their chances were of obtaining a stronger lead, or more information, than they already had.

CHAPTER ELEVEN

"We need to find where he's taken Rosemary," May said in a low voice to Owen, as they waited on the sidewalk. "Or else, taken her body." But she didn't want to accept they were too late. She was still clinging to the hope they'd make a breakthrough, or else one of the police patrols now out on the roads might possibly save her in time.

"How are we going to do that?" he asked. "He couldn't take her to the burial site he uses. Perhaps he's waiting, keeping her somewhere. Surely there's a chance she's still alive?" he added hopefully.

May got on the phone to Sheriff Jack. "Rosemary Pharr has been taken, but we need to find her. She might be kept somewhere overnight. We need to put the word out county-wide."

"I'll do that, May. I'll circulate her description. I'll ask all police departments to do night patrols with all available personnel, and look out for any unusual vehicles, any signs anything is wrong, any sounds of trouble."

"If there's a chance we can find her, we must," May pleaded. "I wish we had more information. But maybe, if someone is alert, they could pick up something that will save her. I'll keep my phone with me. I'll be ready to head out, any time of the night."

"I'll make sure the search is as intensive as possible," Jack promised.

They cut the call. Now there was nothing else May could do but wait for forensics to arrive.

A few cars swished past as they waited, their headlights bright in the gathering dusk. May caught a couple of curious glances as the motorists passed by. She was known to many of the locals, and she was sure they would be wondering why she and her partner were standing there. Especially since, following this news, she knew there would be a spreading sense of fear in the community.

As she puzzled over the killer's movements, a thought occurred to May.

It wasn't a nice thought. In fact, as she stared into Owen's worried eyes, that thought began giving her cold shivers. But it needed to be followed up.

"You know, one of the things I did pick up when we were at the police department?" she asked him in a low voice.

"What?" Owen replied.

"I picked up that one of the women I expected to find in that grave, wasn't there," May said. "Iris Arnold. Remember Iris? Age thirty? She went missing about three years ago."

"I wasn't with the police then. I was still at the accounting firm," Owen said. "But the name is familiar. She's from Tamarack County, isn't she? And went missing here?"

"Yes, but there was a lot of confusion over whether she'd hitchhiked south to try and join her brother as she said she was going to do. And then there was that horrific car wreck on the interstate where a tanker burned. And we ended up theorizing that she'd been in that crash and wasn't able to be identified."

"Yes, now I remember," Owen said.

"Owen, what if she wasn't? What if she was taken by the killer? She could easily have been, and the name matches up with what he would have looked for."

Shivers coursed up and down May's spine again. This was such a horrible line of thought she didn't want to follow it, but knew she had to.

"So, my point is, what if he has more than one burial site?" she asked Owen.

From the way Owen shuddered, she knew that idea was creeping him out, just as much as it was her.

"May that's - that's spine chilling," he said.

"But it might be the case."

"It might be. And if so, if the worst has happened, he could have taken Rosemary somewhere else, or be planning to. But how would we find that site, May?"

May nodded. That was the question. How were they going to find that site?

"I don't know. Unless -"

"Unless?" Owen prompted her.

"Unless we can gain some insight into his mind. Into how he thinks and plans."

"Unless we can get into his head," Owen agreed.

"What were the features of the site? Let's go over them again so we know what his parameters are likely to be."

"Close to a road. I noticed that," Owen said. "I guess that would be so he didn't have to carry the bodies too far."

"And low-lying ground. Not high ground."

"And covered in flowers. I mean, there were a remarkable number of flowers there," Owen observed.

"I guess that makes sense, seeing he's targeting his victims based on their name. At least, that's one of the reasons we know about," May said, feeling uneasily aware that there was still a lot they did not know.

But for a start, they could try to work out where alternative burial grounds might be.

"It would have to be a wild meadow," she said. "Not one used by farmers, or even hikers. Unused land that doesn't have a walking trail going through it."

She felt they were starting to narrow down what had initially felt like an impossible job.

"There are a few areas like that near the lake," she remembered.

"And one other thing," Owen warned.

"What's that?"

"If he's prepared a grave for her and has buried her in that meadow, there will be signs of disturbed ground. Signs of digging. So that will provide us a clue."

"It will," May said, feeling another chill of apprehension.

At that moment, a car pulled up with its blue light flashing. The pathology team had arrived.

Dr. Andy Baker climbed out, his face serious.

"Evening, May," he said. "I can't believe this killer has taken another victim, but I'm glad you picked this up soon. We'll set up here, take samples of whatever we find, and analyze the site."

"Please let me know when you're done," May said. "Here's the details for Rosemary's boyfriend, Chuck. He's expecting you to come by for a DNA sample."

"That's good. I'm glad he's prepared and waiting," Andy said calmly.

With the scene now being forensically examined, May and Owen turned away and trudged back to the mall where they had left their car.

"I guess it's too late now to start looking for meadows," Owen said. "We'd need to work on that during the day, especially to pick up signs of disturbance."

"Yes. That's definitely a project for tomorrow morning," May said. "For now, I guess we could go back to the police department and compile a list of the missing persons with flower names, who haven't turned up so far in the mass grave."

"Yes, I guess that would be helpful. The more of the families we can speak to, the better the chances are that we find something. Surely?" Owen added hopefully.

May wasn't feeling hopeful. She was feeling overwhelmed. She was sure that by tomorrow, the FBI would have arrived and would be on the scene, adding their manpower to the efforts to find the killer.

But then, as they approached her car, May's phone rang. She didn't recognize the number, but picked up immediately.

"Deputy Moore speaking," she said.

"Deputy, it's Mark Gregory here. Lily's older brother."

"Good evening, Mark," May said, wondering why Mark was calling. With Lily having been missing for three weeks, and her body now unearthed, she wondered if Mark might have some information he wanted to share.

Sure enough, her instinct was right.

"My mother said we should call you if we had anything that could possibly help," he explained.

"Yes, we asked her to. Do you have something helpful?"

"Well, yes. For a while, a few months back, she dated a very weird guy. It wasn't for long, they split up quite soon, because like I said, he was weird."

"Weird in what way?" May asked.

"He used to mumble to himself all the time. He sometimes seemed really out of it, like he was on drugs, or actually more like on another planet, I thought. He was hugely secretive and there were times he wouldn't let her visit him. And he had, like, a fetish for flowers, their scents, their colors."

With her phone on speaker, May and Owen glanced excitedly at each other. This could lead somewhere.

"Is that so?"

"Yes. We joked it was why he dated her. For her name. Anyway, he wasn't right for her and I think they ran into problems very soon. But now I'm wondering if he could be linked to this."

"Where can we find him? What's his name?"

"His name's Zane Naylor and he runs a flower shop near the big cemetery outside Chestnut Hill. He lives behind the shop. Lily visited him there a few times and I dropped her off there once. I can send you a pin drop."

"Please do. We'll go there immediately," May said.

She felt as if this case had suddenly taken a giant step forward.

A flower-obsessed, weird ex was exactly the kind of person who could have been committing these murders. Without a doubt, there was a possible link, and there was no time to waste in questioning Zane Naylor.

CHAPTER TWELVE

Although the flower shop would be closed at this time of the evening, May wondered if Zane would be at home, in his apartment behind the shop. She guessed that if he'd taken Rosemary, he would have had enough time to kill her and dump her in a grave that he'd prepared. He would probably be home already, feeling satisfied after successfully murdering her.

At any rate, the minute the pin drop came through, she and Owen powered onto the road, on their way and hoping to find this creepy, flower-obsessed ex who might hold the key to the killings.

"It's a right turn here, then left," Owen said, studying the map as May sped along the road. It was now fully dark.

Ahead, she could see the lights of Chestnut Hill, clustered on the sloping hillside.

As they drew closer, May could see the darker patch among the lights, where the huge graveyard with its winding paths was located.

They drove a short distance and then rounded a corner. The lights above the small row of shops on the street opposite the cemetery entrance were clearly visible. There was a coffee shop, a laundromat, a grocer, and of course, the flower shop.

"Yes. It's there," Owen said.

It was called Floral Obsessions, May noted with narrowed eyes. Was there another clue waiting for them in that name?

The shops themselves, at this hour, were all dark and locked up. It gave the center a desolate feeling. May parked in one of the empty spaces outside.

It looked as if the small apartments backed onto the stores, but that you had to walk around to access them. May paced around the corner of the center, hoping that they would get lucky and find their suspect.

Her heart accelerated when she saw that a faint light was on in the apartment that backed onto the flower store.

"It looks like Zane's at home," she said, feeling a thrill of determination that they were going to be able to come face to face with this suspect in another short minute.

May walked up to the apartment door. Unlike the stores at the front, which were neatly maintained and in good condition, the apartment behind the shop was definitely less so.

The brickwork was pitted, and the front door was in need of a sand and varnish. There was a strange smell in the air, which May couldn't place, but it was not a smell that she associated with flowers.

She'd imagined a pretty apartment, with geranium pots outside. That had been her vision for this flower obsessed man. But this was creepier and seedier and she wondered if it reflected the true character of the man who lived here.

She knocked on the door.

Footsteps approached. And then the door opened to reveal a man in his mid-thirties with a pale, moon-like face, dark hair, and dark eyes. He wore faded jeans and a white T-shirt. His expression was strangely blank, and he didn't appear surprised to see them. It was hard to make out much more because the overhead light in the hall was either turned off, or not working.

"Zane Naylor?" May asked. Was that a muddy footprint on the floor? She narrowed her eyes, trying to see it better in the dim light.

He nodded.

May's first thought was whether this man was old enough to have committed the murders. She decided he was. If he'd started young, his approximate age fit the time span they were seeking.

"Deputies Moore and Lovell. We'd like to ask you a couple of questions," she said.

She couldn't tell from his expression what he was thinking. Zane was not giving anything away.

"Can we come in?"

Now, she saw his eyes flicker.

"Can you come in? Sure, sure, of course. You can. Come in. Yes."

May blinked. This was certainly the strangest offer of entry into premises she'd yet had.

Zane led the way through the dark and narrow hall. From there, he veered right, into a small room that was also dark, May saw to her confusion.

"In here. In here, please, we can talk. In here. Please."

"Is there a light?" May asked, confused, as Zane waved them in.

"Yes. There is. A light. It's down the passage. I'll go. And switch it on. I'll switch it on for you."

He just about shoved Owen into the room.

Then, as Owen was fumbling in his pocket to get out his phone flashlight, May heard a click behind them and the room got suddenly even darker.

She spun around.

The impossible realization dawned on her that Zane had closed the door, with him on the other side. Gasping in surprise, May heard the metallic scrabble of the key in the lock.

She felt utterly shocked at this sound, and for a moment, her brain could not actually take in what was happening.

And then, in a rush, she realized what his devious plan had been, one they had never expected in their surprise as he'd ushered them inside.

"He's locking us in!"

She dove for the door, at exactly the same moment Owen snapped on the flashlight.

But May was too late. She twisted the handle, but it wouldn't open.

They were in Zane's bedroom, she realized in astonishment, turning around to look at what the flashlight revealed. That was where he'd led them to. It contained a double bed with a dip in the mattress and a scuffed gray duvet, a chest of drawers that was partway open, with socks and underwear spilling out, and a small cupboard that had one door hanging off the hinges and looked to be crammed with clothes and bags.

The stale smell of the room was somewhat offset by the massive arrangement of flowers on the bedside table. A few days old, the roses, chrysanthemums, and gladioli were drooping and losing their petals.

A bookcase in the corner of the room was cluttered with books on botany, flowers, cultivars, and bulbs. On the walls were amateurish, hand-drawn sketches of various blooms. Most definitely, this man was both weird, and flower-obsessed.

"Let us out!" May yelled. But there was no reply from beyond the door. She heard another door slam. That sounded like the front door, and adrenaline surged inside her as she realized what move he'd pulled.

This man was definitely not normal. His behavior was highly suspicious. And now, he'd locked them in and was without a doubt going to use this window of time to make his escape.

"We need to get out, before he gets away," May spluttered, appalled that he had managed to pull this move on them so sneakily.

"Stand back, May," Owen said, his voice urgent. "Let me see if I can break through the door."

May squeezed away, pressing herself against the edge of the bed, as her deputy lined himself up on the far side of the room and took a running jump at the door, his feet thudding on the worn carpet. Determination was in his eyes as he leaped for the door, his foot lashing forward in a perfect kick.

He hit the lock squarely with the ball of his left foot and to May's relief, the door shattered open, the wooden jamb breaking at the handle with a cracking sound.

Feeling full of admiration at that perfectly executed lock smash, May burst through the doorway.

"Zane Naylor!" she yelled.

But there was no reply. She hadn't expected one. He'd run from them, and now the only question in her mind was where he'd gone.

He must have gone out, she decided. No way would someone this sneaky be hiding inside the house, she thought. He would not be wanting to lay low, but rather to get away, and he must have run into the parking lot, looking to get as much distance between him and the police as he could.

"We need to get him! We need to find him!"

May rushed to the door and burst out of the apartment, staring around her in the darkening night. Where was he? Which direction had he fled?

Then, from the right, a flash of movement caught her eye. Was that him?

She thought it was. That glimpse of white had been his shirt. Zane was running for it, as fast as he could, around the right-hand side of the building.

They had to stop him and they had to outwit a man who was clearly far sneakier and more desperate than they had given him credit for at first.

Scenarios flashed through May's mind in an instant as she considered what the best option would be.

"I'll go right, and follow him!" she said to Owen.

He nodded. "I'll go left, and cut him off if he tries to double back," he said.

With their hasty plan in mind, May set off, racing as fast as she could go across the slippery and uneven paving, hoping that they could catch up with Zane and take him down, before the sneaky and highly suspicious man managed to evade their clutches.

CHAPTER THIRTEEN

May raced around the side of the small apartment block, desperate to keep Zane in her sight, or at any rate, to catch up with where he was fleeing, before he disappeared or hid. As she ran, she was already checking off the options in her mind as to where he might go.

His car. Did he have a car? If he did, it wouldn't be at the front of the building. So he wasn't running for a car.

That must mean he had some other idea about where to go, some bolt hole that he planned to use, or else an escape route that would allow him to dodge out of sight.

Of course, he could also be running blindly in a panic. That would be the better option for May and Owen, because there would be less risk that he'd evade them. Running blindly was the best case scenario for them, for sure.

Her shoes skidded on the worn paving stones, and her foot banged painfully into the side of the wall as she hurtled around the corner. But May's own momentum powered her forward and she flung her legs ahead of her, regaining her balance as she stared into the darkness to see where he was.

There he was, ahead, racing across the road. The flash of white caught her eye once again and she locked onto it, narrowing her gaze in the shadowy dark, waiting for the moments when the street lights or the outside lights of houses illuminated that shirt, which was really the only part of Zane she had a hope of seeing.

A thudding of footsteps to her left told her that Owen was on the chase. She didn't expect her deputy to join her directly. Owen was a master at guesswork when it came to fleeing suspects. And he knew the area well. He would probably be trying to anticipate Zane's moves, taking the circular route or the side alley, while May kept running after him directly.

Where was he going? May pounded across the road after him, her shoes thudding on the blacktop, feeling glad that at this hour the road was quiet. It was Saturday night, and people were heading into the main parts of town, not making for this quiet, backwater area with its peaceful cemetery and quiet local shopping complex.

She had the feeling that Zane was running in a panic. He didn't seem to be making for any hiding place. How could he be, when he was racing along the road as if trying to exceed a human land-speed limit? And that was the problem, she realized, her lungs burning as she gasped in air for the pursuit. He was fast, and motivated, and clearly wanted to escape them at all costs.

May couldn't let that happen. She felt her shoes thudding on the blacktop as she did her best to outrun this man, who was worryingly long-legged and fleeing from them as if his life depended on it.

And what if it did, May thought, adrenaline flooding her veins as she tried to pick up her pace another gear. What if this man was running because he knew he was guilty, and that if he was caught, they would find he had committed all these heinous crimes?

That made her even more determined to catch him, but he seemed hell bent on getting away. Now, he was veering down a side street, disappearing from her view so that her stomach lurched. She thought she guessed what his strategy was. Seeing it was now totally dark, he was going to try and avoid the bigger roads with street lights, and head into the darker areas.

If he got any more of a lead, they would lose him. And with so much at stake, they could not afford to do that right now.

"Stop! Police!" May yelled into the darkness, just in case it made a difference, or somebody ahead might hear and help them.

It didn't. There was nobody ahead, nobody in sight at all. He completely ignored her screamed request to stop, and ran off even faster into the narrow, twisting roads behind the graveyard.

And now, May saw, he was running along the graveyard road itself. She could hear the regular thump-thump of his footsteps. But she caught no more than the barest glimpse of that shirt, because he was now far ahead, and gaining. He was running with all the speed of desperation and she felt a flare of panic that she wouldn't catch him, that he had bought enough time and distance to be able to get away and hide.

"Stop!" she yelled again, hoping that even if her shouted plea didn't have an effect on the fugitive, it might just alert someone nearby who could join the chase.

But it was Saturday night, people were indoors, having showers, getting ready with hairdryers blasting before going out, or parked in front of the television for a night of microwave meals.

Nobody was out on the streets at this hour. Nobody was listening to hear the drama unfolding in their neighborhood. There was nobody to help May catch up with this potentially murderous man who was clearly running for a reason.

Where was Owen? The thought flashed through her mind. Only her deputy could help her catch up with this fleeing fugitive from justice.

Perhaps she could distract Zane, May thought suddenly, if she could find any breath to call to him. It was worth a try. Anything right now was worth a try.

"You're going to be in big trouble," she yelled.

That didn't have an effect at all. He didn't even pause.

"You're going to spend a lot of time in jail." May wished her burning lungs would allow her to elaborate on her ideas. But at least she was trying to get through to him, as she raced behind him down the quiet suburban lane.

"We're going to go back and search your house!" she tried, in a last-ditch attempt to have something work.

And at that moment, ahead of her, May thought she'd caught a gap.

She saw a sudden glimpse of movement as the white-shirted figure fleeing ahead of her suddenly stumbled hard, as if those words had startled him and thrown him right off balance. She heard the scrape and scrabble of footsteps as he fought to right himself.

And then, she saw the sight she'd been waiting and hoping for.

From the park to the right, pounding down the paved running track, Owen burst out and headed directly for Zane.

Zane had gotten his balance back, but not his speed. Accelerating toward him, May saw him veer indecisively. He feinted left and right.

Then he turned, ready to flee, and stared in horror as he saw her approach. She was clearly much closer than he'd expected her to be.

While he was still frozen in surprise, Owen reached him and grabbed him from behind.

Zane let out a frantic yell as Owen's hand closed around the back of his white T-shirt.

He was captured. At last, on this dark and deserted street, they'd managed to locate the fleeing fugitive.

They were all breathing hard. May felt dizzy from lack of air, but she couldn't let that stop her from gasping out a warning to the captured suspect.

"You have to – cooperate with us – now. You are – going to be questioned – in connection with a series of crimes."

Breathing equally hard, Owen added to the warning.

"Do not try to escape again."

May didn't think he could. The headlong flight seemed to have taken everything out of Zane. He simply nodded, stooped, and gasped for breath as May and Owen grabbed an arm each, and escorted him back down the surprisingly long route that they'd run.

May couldn't wait to question him as soon as they were inside his apartment. There had to be a reason for his instant, instinctive guilt. She hoped she could get to the truth of it, and find out if this man was their killer.

CHAPTER FOURTEEN

Returning to Zane's dark and dingy apartment, May headed straight through the darkened hall, bypassing the bedroom, hoping to find a lounge or somewhere they could sit down and question this suspect.

She snapped on a light on the wall and saw a bulb glow dimly. And ahead was a lounge – of sorts, anyway, which was better lit than the rest of the apartment.

"Let's sit in here," she called to Owen, who was following behind, still holding tightly onto Zane.

Now, the flower shop owner looked apprehensive and scared as they sat him down in the scantily furnished room, which contained one battered settee and two ragged armchairs, as well as a very large TV. May saw discarded popcorn packets and a box that might have contained a hamburger.

There were more amateur drawings of flowers on the walls. For the first time, she noticed there was a rose embroidered on the pocket of his white shirt.

"Zane Naylor, you fled from police. In fact, you locked us into your apartment and tried to escape us. You have some answers to give us," May said firmly. "You need to explain your actions, and then you need to give us the background we came to find out."

"Background?"

"Yes. We came here to question you about Lily, your ex-girlfriend. She was recently found dead. That's why we're here now."

"Dead?" Zane's mouth was half open. He was snorting slightly through his nose as he stared at May and Owen. May was worried by a strange blankness in his eyes. What was happening with this man? Why was he only responding so far by repeating what May had said? Was he deliberately trying to evade their questions?

May thought through all the possibilities as she gazed at their suspect sternly. She did not want to show any signs of weakness or worry, but she had to admit she was concerned by the way he was drooping sideways, in a manner that brought to mind a wilted flower.

Had the headlong run exhausted him, was he short of oxygen, did he have a medical condition they weren't aware of? She didn't want to be responsible for having their suspect rushed to hospital.

But then, May thought again.

This was no medical condition. His eyes were too bloodshot for that.

"Mr. Naylor," she said firmly, hoping that she could bring him back to reality if her voice was sharp enough. Kerry seemed to have that ability, naturally. May had noticed it when watching her sister questioning suspects. A certain edge to the voice, and everyone sat up straight and paid attention.

May did her best to give her words that same cutting, icy tone. "You need to answer us, and answer us now."

"Yeah? Okay, okay. What do you want to know?" His voice was slightly slurred. He swayed in his seat.

This wasn't exhaustion, May was beginning to realize. This was something else. Their suspect was as high as a kite.

But with time pressing down on them, they would just have to struggle along and do their best with what they had, which was a rather incoherent man.

"Firstly, your relationship with Lily. How long did you date for?"

"Lily?" he asked, swaying again.

"Lily Gregory," May snapped.

He stared at her blankly. "But that was – that was long ago and we didn't really date. We just – we just spent some time together. She met me here, at the shop. Flowers are my thing, you see. I love them. She came in to buy a bouquet and we got to talking. Then we saw each other a few times."

"And then?"

"No, it didn't work out."

"Why's that?" May probed.

"I was too busy, with the shop and all. I spend time here, you see. Flowers, they fascinate me. They're my hobby and my work." He almost fell over on the couch, but righted himself with a startle.

"Who broke it off?"

"She did," he said reluctantly.

"And were you angry about that? Did you try and contact her again?"

"Yeah, I called her a few times. But then I left it. You see, flowers are my thing, really. They're my thing."

May was getting intensely frustrated. It felt like she was questioning this man through a fog. But she had no choice but to press on. At least he was able to speak.

She thought back to the time that Lily had disappeared. Three weeks ago, on a Thursday afternoon.

"Are you the only person who works in this shop?" she asked, wanting to know if he was the sole employee.

"No. I have help. There's a lady, who comes in to help on a Tuesday and Wednesday. Sometimes other days, too. When I need to go out. Or else I just close the shop, you see, if people need flowers, they can always just come back. That's my thinking. They can come back."

"Did you work here today?" May asked, wondering if he'd closed up shop early so that he could go and grab Rosemary. Perhaps he'd indulged in something highly illegal after his murderous efforts.

"Today, I was here. Saturday is busy. I make a lot of sales, I mean, a lot of sales. I only closed my doors after five. People came to buy flowers. That's my thing."

"Can you prove you were here?"

"Prove? You need me to prove? I – I guess I can prove. Yeah, I can prove all my transactions. I have an electronic till and it keeps records of everything. It keeps records of all the sales. And all the times."

He shrugged heavily. His eyelids drooped.

May felt a flash of disappointment that the till would provide the proof that they needed to clear him, even though she was not going to take his word for it, and would check it thoroughly, and if possible even follow up with some customers to check who had attended to them.

But she had the sudden feeling he was about to fall asleep, despite the tenseness of the situation. And yet, if he was so innocent, why had he acted so strangely when they'd arrived? If the till provided all the answers, why had they been made to run what felt like miles in the dark, trying to catch this man?

"Why did you run from us?" she asked.

Zane shook his head. He lurched to one side and then hurriedly righted himself.

"No reason. All good." He gave her a big wide smile.

But May thought back to that frenzied chase, and the question she'd yelled to him that had finally caused this man to break stride and stumble.

She'd shouted out that they were going to search his apartment. And that had been what had made him lose his footing.

"Owen, could you wait here a moment," May said.

She wanted to explore this apartment further, despite the fact that her suspect was now all but comatose on the couch. She wanted to find out if there was another reason for his guilt and his need to flee.

Owen moved over to the couch and grasped Zane firmly by the arm again. While he did that, May got up and walked out of the door.

The apartment was very small. It was just the lounge, the kitchenette, and that messy bedroom. May guessed that they could search the bedroom for drugs, but even if Zane was not thinking clearly, he surely would not have locked two police officers in a room with his stash.

If he was doing anything untoward, May guessed it would be elsewhere.

She remembered seeing a stairway going down to a basement room. Perhaps there was something down there that could give her more of a clue.

She walked back to the hall, and took the narrow stairs down. The smell was stronger here, for sure. Something was going on. What was he keeping in this underground room?

The hairs on May's neck stood up and she felt suddenly spooked.

At the bottom of the stairs was a closed door.

She pushed it open, and caught her breath, staring in horror at the sight that met her eyes.

Down here, in this basement room, which was much larger than it seemed, Zane Naylor had set up an entire greenhouse. Lights shimmered from the ceiling. The dank smell of water and mildew filled the air. And May's eyes widened as she realized the room was filled with beds of poppies.

He was farming heroin.

A highly illegal, highly addictive drug operation was taking place in the basement. She could barely breathe as she looked around, taking in the details of this illicit activity.

Zane might not be their killer, but he was a criminal who was ruining many lives with his underground operations.

They needed to call in the local police urgently, arrest this man, charge him, and shut down the operation.

Criminal as he was, though, Zane hadn't committed the crimes that they had suspected him of. He'd been in his flower shop, selling floral arrangements and heroin to customers. He hadn't had the opportunity, or the coherence, to organize the killings.

He'd run because he'd thought they were going to discover what he was doing in his basement, and not because he was a murderer.

It was now close to ten p.m. and May felt weighted down by tiredness and discouragement as she ascended the stairs. They were still no closer to tracking down Rosemary's body or finding the killer.

As she trailed outside the apartment, ready to get on the radio to the Chestnut Hill police, May knew that she was going to pursue this case in the morning with all the energy she had. This killer might be a local, and know all the paths and hiding places, but so was she.

Before dawn tomorrow, they were going to embark on the hunt for Rosemary's grave, to see if there was another concealed burial site that this prolific killer was using. And May had a few ideas where they could start.

CHAPTER FIFTEEN

He could pick up that scent from a mile away. It was as if it wafted to him through the air. The floral notes, the hint of musk, the fruity overtones of rose. He knew its name. It was a beautiful scent for sure, although not as strongly connected to him as the one he needed to use, and would use on her when the time was right.

She was a beautiful girl. Her name was Primrose Eliot, and at this moment, she was getting ready to go out on the town.

The hunter knew Primrose well. After all, he'd been observing her for weeks. He'd been waiting for the time to be right - for her, but also for him.

He knew her routine. She was a college girl, so she was up with the sun and attending class. She had a part-time job as a waitress at the Bluebird Grill, and she had dance classes which she attended twice a week. She was busy, but she had plenty of free time, and she was often on her own too.

But he had not yet had the right opportunity to grab her. Every time it was as if she'd been strangely blessed by fate, or cursed, depending on how you looked at it.

The killer had not done his job for more than a decade without learning the art of patience. Never mind that. It had been taught to him when he was younger. Locked away in a dark room for days, he had learned the art for himself, and it was no wonder he found it so easy now.

"Oh, you evil little boy. I'm going to hurt you now, because you deserve it."

The harsh voice he remembered from his childhood, the cutting words that had lashed at him like a whip, and the cruel punishments that followed. All of these loomed in his mind and he knew that they could never be fully defeated.

But they could be chased away. That was what he had to do. He'd been unable to do it when he was younger. He'd suffered the full fury of the monster woman and her abuse. He remembered those days without food, vicious beatings, being locked away in a darkened cellar.

He remembered the scuttling sound of rats, invisible in the gloom, and how he'd feared that they would be drawn to the fresh blood on his back and his arms. From the wounds she'd inflicted before imprisoning him there.

"Please, no," he'd begged, in a broken voice, but she never seemed to hear. In fact, he wondered sometimes if his own begging had made her even angrier and even more intent on inflicting the most painful punishment she could.

And he remembered how she'd smelled, the scent and fragrance of her skin. The signature perfume she wore had always seemed associated with the demons that she'd left him with.

He had to keep their presence at bay and he knew that the perfume – that specific scent, was a vital part of the ritual.

He had created a reserve of potential prey. One that he could draw on, when the monsters came and the need arose. The names of women were easy to find. They were on social media, or out in the public domain, sometimes even on the name badges they wore for work. He had a long list, and he always chose names associated with flowers, because they were the most significant for him and he knew they fed his monsters the best.

He had some private wealth; he didn't need to work. That was the only benefit his mother had left him with. Generational wealth and a trust fund. So his work was what he did now, which was recovering from her cruelty by slaying his demons again and again.

And it was a full time job to do what he did, without being caught, without being seen, over and over. It was not what he would have chosen, but he accepted that it was what he needed.

Tonight, it looked as if he would get his chance with the beautiful Primrose. She was off and away, to meet friends, he guessed. He'd been careful to stay at a distance, not to look at her too closely. It was a warm evening, and she wore a floral summer dress that bared her shoulders and much of her back.

She was walking outside to wait for a cab. And he was parked nearby, in the driver's seat, ready to accelerate toward her, stop, jump out, take her.

That was what he craved. The hunt, the chase, the kill, and the final confrontation with his demons. It was such a good feeling when they subsided. It was his calling, what he needed to do. His obsession, his compulsion, his reason for living.

His list gave him comfort. He would spend days looking for new names to add to it. Research was important and it energized him to do it. It comforted him to know there would always be somebody to hunt, when the clamoring of his demons grew too loud.

They were never completely subdued. He knew that.

And that brought another flash of fear to him, because there was another factor that might allow them to destroy him down the line. It was one he had no control over. He'd only realized the bombshell when the fragrance he needed, which was extremely costly, had not been available.

It was deeply worrying. Ever since he had known about this potential disaster, the hunter had found himself more anxious. And anxiety flared his demons, so he'd had to create his scenarios to destroy them more often than usual.

But as yet, he was not ready to inhale that smell he needed. Instead, he was waiting patiently, because the first step in the process was to claim his prey.

His car was a late model SUV that was unremarkable apart from its bright color, which he liked, because it reminded him of blood, and of sacrifice, and of some of his favorite flowers.

Now, the hunter got out of the car and made his way toward the apartment block.

He was pleased that he'd picked this place. It meant he had an easy getaway. There was nothing to stop him from following his prey and striking when she was alone. He knew exactly where she would walk, the path she would take from the side of her apartment, around the building, to wait for the cab.

But she always arrived early, that he had seen. During his patient observation of her, he'd noticed that, and he had known it would give him the chance that he needed.

She would always be out and waiting minutes before the cab pulled up. He didn't know why. Perhaps in the past, an impatient cab driver had driven away and left her without a ride. Or maybe she was naturally a very punctual person. But outside, and in the dark, would be the perfect opportunity.

He smiled. He was ready. He was always ready. He'd been ready to hunt her for a long time and felt pleased that tonight, she would be the one to satiate his demons. His patience had finally been rewarded. He was sure that this woman would keep them at bay for a while, and return to him his fragile feeling of peace.

It's going to be a good night, he thought. And he would make it as beautiful as he could.

He would make it a place of flowers.

He would make it a place of death.

CHAPTER SIXTEEN

There was an intruder in May's room, and her blood turned to ice as she realized this fact, and felt the intent of his unfriendly presence. She could hear the implacable footsteps approaching her bed, and the hiss of his soft breathing. Despite the cameras, despite the new security gate on her bedroom door, someone had gotten in.

She couldn't see him as he had on a dark, hooded jacket. All she could pick up was the glint of his eyes as he stared at her.

She sat bolt upright in the bed and stared at the dark figure. Her heart was beating like a drum and her head felt light.

"I told you to back off, May Moore," the stranger - she guessed it was a man in his thirties or forties - hissed at her as he approached. He was tall, taller than she'd thought. He loomed over her, powerful and threatening and yet, utterly anonymous.

She wanted to scream, to alert a neighbor to his presence, but she found it impossible to speak. She had no voice.

"I've been watching you, even though you don't think I have been," he continued. "I told you not to ask any more questions about Lauren. You aren't listening. And now, you will pay the price."

The intruder stepped up to the bed and grabbed May's arm. His fingers were cold and strong, his grasp icy. He was going to take her. This was it.

Finally May found the voice to scream. She screamed at the top of her voice, shrieked in terror.

She screamed herself right out of the nightmare, realizing that her full scale cries of terror had been nothing more than breathy whimpers.

Her bedroom was empty, and the faintest light of morning was filtering through the curtain.

May was breathing fast. Terror still surged inside her as she sat up, staring around and making sure there was nobody watching. A cold sweat prickled her spine. She'd had that nightmare a few times now, since someone had left those threats on her laptop. Every time, it felt more real than actual reality, and utterly petrifying.

She wondered if Kerry would make anything of the video. Probably not, she thought. She guessed she'd found everything that there was to be found from it. She'd really sent it more to help her sister and distract her from the pain of the break-up. And also to share with her what she was doing, because that was only fair.

Today, she was sure, Kerry would be arriving with the FBI team. They would help them with this case.

But for now, it was getting light, and that meant that it was time for the arrangement May had made with Owen yesterday. They were going to go and scope out a few of the most likely sites where this killer might have dumped his bodies.

She checked her phone again, just in case there was news on Rosemary, but there was nothing. Clearly, the overnight searches hadn't made progress.

May scrambled out of bed and dressed quickly. She made sure to lock her bedroom door behind her after she left the room, and made extra sure that the house was securely locked up when she stepped out of the front door. The chilly tendrils of that dream were still clinging to her mind.

She got into her car and drove to the police department, Since it was just five minutes away, she knew she would arrive there at exactly five a.m.

Even though they were starting at this early hour, May feared that the killer had already done his work. She had the terrible image of Rosemary's body lying in a shallow grave.

But they were going to find her, whatever it took. He was not going to hide this new victim away for months and years. And then, they were going to find him. This slaughter, this murder, was going to stop, May resolved, as she braked and pulled over outside the police department.

At that moment, Owen's car pulled up behind hers and parked in one of the spaces outside the building. Her deputy got out and jogged over to her car. May was impressed by how wide awake he looked for having gotten such an early start. And better still, he was holding a large flask of coffee.

"Morning, May," he greeted her, climbing into the car.

"Morning, Owen," she said.

She looked at him, and her face warmed into a smile. With him there, everything seemed better. The aroma of coffee filled the space as he poured it into two mugs.

May slurped a big gulp of coffee gratefully. Caffeine was sorely needed. Between that and Owen's company, the day already felt brighter. She felt ready to cope with what was surely going to be a difficult task.

"I've thought of a few places where we could look," Owen said. "I brought a map along."

"Me, too," May said. "How about we mark off on the map where we think he could have taken the bodies, and if there are any places we both think likely, we go there first?"

"Great idea," Owen said.

He unfolded a large scale paper map of the area, and he and May both took a pen.

May smoothed out the top left corner of the map. She identified the road she had thought of. It was a pretty country lane that ran in between small farms, with tracts of wood on either side. There were several wild meadows along its route, but May had narrowed the possibilities down to two that she would have chosen if she were the killer, based on the fact they were low lying, and close to the road.

She shaded them both in carefully.

Then she moved to the bottom left-hand side of the map, where there was another possibility toward the south. And finally, she leaned over to Owen's side, and shaded in the two places that were north of town. One was near a small tributary of Eagle Lake. The other was among farmland further to the west. It was bordered by a hiking trail but May didn't think the trail crossed that particular part of open ground that was always bright with flowers at this time of year.

She waited for Owen to finish, and then took a look at what they had.

There were two sections of the map that they'd both chosen.

One was the very first meadow that May had colored in, and the other was the one near the tributary of Eagle Lake.

"Well, we have two in common," she said.

"Which one shall we pick first?" Owen asked.

"I guess the closer one. And then drive to the one that's further away."

"Good idea. That site near the lake is only a couple of miles away."

May gulped down the rest of her coffee. Then she started the car and drove out of town, heading to the small, scenic tributary of Eagle Lake that curved around the town to the south.

At this early hour, the roads were quiet and there were only one or two other cars along the route. May found herself looking at them suspiciously. In the back of her mind she was wondering if one of them was the killer, freshly returned from his gruesome job.

The sky was brightening, and May guessed the sun would rise in another few minutes. It was going to be a glorious summer Sunday.

And she was going to spend it pursuing this man, who had been allowed to cause so much grief and destruction for years.

Here was the meadow, colorfully studded with flowers. They got out and stood by the side of the road, looking down at it. It was an easy and convenient site to get to, with the road winding past it and the lake glimmering beyond. May felt that the killer might have been drawn to it. But even though May and Owen paced along the road, she couldn't see any signs of disturbed earth.

"There's nothing in sight here," Owen said, echoing the thoughts she had.

May nodded grimly. "That means Rosemary's body wasn't dumped here. Let's go to the other site we both chose, and then start looking at the others."

For a moment, she felt a pang of fear that she was on the totally wrong track. But this time, May didn't allow herself to get caught up in it. As they drove in silence to the next site, she managed to stop the uncertainty from taking over. Drawing in a deep breath, she refused to let herself fall prey to her usual anxiety. She was on the right track and needed to believe in herself.

For once, she needed to force herself to be more like Kerry and less like the part of herself that she hated.

With the roads free of traffic so early on a Sunday morning, the drive was very quick, and only a few minutes later, May reached the site. She parked and climbed out, thinking how similar it was to the previous site. A breeze was starting up, and the morning was fresh, and already warming. She paced over to the small meadow and gazed down, her eyes searching the flowery grass for any sign of disturbance.

And May drew in a gasp as she saw what they were looking for. She heard Owen murmur something, shocked words that she barely heard.

A big, rectangular scar was visible amid the flowers. Fresh earth had been shoveled aside. She could almost smell the dampness of the soil from here. Shivers coursed through her as she stared at the proof. The proof that another woman had lost her life and been hastily buried here, just hours ago.

"We need to get the teams out," May said firmly, trying her best to sound strong, rather than shocked. "This is a fresh site. And we have to find something, Owen. This kill is so recent, there must be a clue. I am sure there will be something on this site or on the body that will tell us more about him."

CHAPTER SEVENTEEN

Owen felt utterly shocked at the scale of these kills. It chilled his blood to think that for years, for decades, this monster had been picking off victims from among the local towns.

Doing it so skillfully that nobody had noticed a pattern. But clearly there was a very important pattern. Owen felt filled with anger and resolve to hunt this man down, whatever it took. Slowly, he knew, this man would be leaving clues that they could find, now that they knew about him and were hot on his trail.

Flowers. The victims were all named after flowers. They were buried in floral meadows.

There might be other factors and Owen knew he needed to look out for them, even though he didn't yet know what they would be.

As he watched the first cars arrive on the horizon, silhouetted against the rising sun, Owen was sure that other signs would be there. This guy was clearly a psycho. Murdering women because of their names? He'd known to expect the unexpected when he'd joined the police, but he'd never thought he'd be rubbing up against this level of crazy.

But he guessed it existed. Even in his previous life as an accountant, they'd had some pretty weird clients, who had liked doing very creative and highly illegal things with their businesses and their books. Not to mention the things he'd heard about their personal lives – and these were supposedly 'normal' people who had no criminal record.

But this man was the worst kind of criminal, and it made Owen feel sad that the innocent had to suffer so that he could continue feeding his flawed fantasies. He was determined to do everything he could to bring this creepy killer to justice.

Because that was why people joined the police, right? For the purpose of stopping the perpetrators of such crimes, of making the world a safer and more secure place.

"Here they are," May said, sounding pleased as the first two cars sped up to the site, and stopped with a squeal of brakes.

She'd called the relevant people immediately, and Owen had been impressed by how fast and efficiently she'd managed to get the teams into action.

Owen felt a surge of gratitude towards her for how efficient and professional she was. May was calm and in control, she took charge, making sure that everything was organized. She was using every ounce of her background and training.

She'd also requested that a separate team of pathologists go to the other field that May and Owen had both chosen, and examine it for any remains. Owen thought that was a good idea, given that the field was so conveniently situated and so similar to the other two sites. And the team here included Andy Baker, who Owen had the deepest respect for.

As he saw the brown-haired coroner climb out of his van, he felt hopeful that his expertise could shed more light on this case.

"Morning, May. Morning, Owen," Andy said. "This is turning into something of a disaster."

He looked short on sleep. Owen was sure he'd worked late into the night, doing his best to identify the oldest remains, to match them up to missing people and ensure that the families could at least get closure as soon as possible.

Two more police officers from the Fairshore department climbed out of the following car.

"The FBI is arriving in an hour. They're going to meet with Sheriff Jack, who will brief them," the younger of the two, Deputy Hartley, told May.

"Thanks," she nodded.

"They're also bringing a forensic team and hopefully more equipment and resources to help process these sites. Do you know, are there just these two sites? You mentioned the other team is also going to check out a third?" He asked the question with a note of trepidation.

Owen saw May shake her head. "We don't know yet. We have to suspect the worst."

Owen couldn't help biting his lip as he saw Andy Baker, now swathed in PPE, descending the hill slope to the flowery lowland below.

Even though the idea of staring at a freshly buried body made his skin crawl, Owen knew he had to help. If Andy had the courage to do this, he did, too.

He pulled on a head cover, gloves, and foot covers, before slipping and slithering his way down the dew-damp grass, his plastic foot covers offering no purchase. He just about skied to the bottom, waving his arms frantically to stop from overturning. Then, at a more sensible walking pace, he picked his way through the flowers to the area of disturbed earth.

The pathologist was unpacking a kit bag containing a small spade.

He dug it carefully into the earth. Owen watched, wide eyed, as he gently loosened the soil. He knew there was a body under here, and that nothing must be done to damage it.

Having gotten rid of some of the soil, Andy began brushing the rest away with careful hands.

Owen caught his breath as the face he'd been expecting to see appeared. There she was, this poor woman who'd been working at the mall, only to be grabbed and killed.

"Looks like a hard blow to the head," Andy murmured as if to himself. "And then, from the slight bruising I can see around the mouth, I'm guessing that these women were smothered with something soft."

Owen felt a spark of relief that, at least, Rosemary and the others had not had to suffer in pain and terror. Not that it made it any better to steal their lives away so brutally, but a prolonged suffering would have made this unbearable to cope with. As it was, he could keep his gaze on the corpse - just.

"Fresh," Andy commented. "About twelve hours old." He glanced up at them. "I will have a more precise estimation in the lab, but this is just being on the safe side, okay?"

"Sure," May nodded. She, too, had gotten dressed in PPE and come to help - literally, in the trenches. "Thanks, Andy."

Owen felt a lump in his throat. He'd worked with Andy a few times now, and he'd always respected the man's courtesy and calmness. Now, that seemed even more appropriate and necessary. Rosemary looked so beautiful, apart from the wound on her head. Her makeup was still in place. She was still wearing the top she'd clearly put on for her day's work in the mall.

"I said smothered," Andy murmured to himself. "But I'm wondering if there was chloroform, or something, involved here. I smell something, for sure."

He bent closer to the corpse, sniffing.

Then he turned to Owen. "Can you pick up anything?"

Owen's eyes widened. He had to stop himself from flinching back. He was being asked to smell - to actually smell - a corpse?

What would his mother think if she could see him now, he wondered, deciding this was definitely one work moment that would not be shared at family dinners.

Hesitantly, he leaned forward, not wanting to contaminate the scene by removing his mask, but holding it an inch away from his nose so he could try and pick up what Andy was telling him.

"Yes," he said, sounding surprised. "I can pick it up but my nose is not as good as yours. It smells more like perfume to me, not like a chemical. Like quite a strong, intense perfume. Is it coming from her skin or her clothing? It seems to be everywhere."

Andy nodded. "I agree. Now that you've picked it up, it is a strong perfume."

"Didn't she work for one of the department stores, promoting the perfumes?" Owen asked.

"That might account for it. But it definitely is a powerful smell. Perhaps she was demonstrating some, or she used some."

"No, she couldn't have done that," May said. And then, Owen remembered, with a flash of insight, why that was so.

"No, she couldn't. Her boyfriend, Chuck, said yesterday that she was allergic. She couldn't wear it at all. So the killer must have poured it onto her skin and clothes. There's no other way we'd get that smell coming off of her."

Owen was beginning to suspect that they had another piece of the puzzle, thanks to being able to examine this corpse so soon.

Perfume played a role.

"It's definitely strong," May said. "I can smell it from here." She stepped cautiously forward, taking a deeper inhalation. "So he must be using it, or drawn to it, or involved with it in some way. It's clearly significant to him. It's a signature, for sure."

They now knew something they didn't know before. And perhaps this could give them an insight into who he was, when looking at past victims. Had any of them worked with perfume? Dated a perfume manufacturer? Had any incident where perfume was mentioned?

Since it seemed to intertwine with the floral theme, and might possibly play a role, Owen decided this was now where they needed to look.

They had to search back into the past again, armed with yet another piece of evidence that might lead them to the killer's present whereabouts.

CHAPTER EIGHTEEN

May was crowded together with Owen at the desk, head to head, so close their knees were touching as they started on their important new angle of research. This was because the back office at the Fairshore police department was packed.

There were at least ten local police in the admittedly limited space. And there were now four FBI agents there, although she hadn't yet seen Kerry, and guessed she was spearheading the action outside, or at one of the sites.

The feeling of ambition, drive and adrenaline was almost overpowering. An entire team of professionals was uniting and combining in their efforts to catch a man who was horrifying the wider community more with every fresh - or not so fresh - body discovered.

May was trying to shut out the bustle and the hype and the shouted words of, "Yes! They have discovered a body at that third site!"

She was barely aware that the touch of Owen's knee against hers felt strangely good, and as if it was something she didn't want to stop or move away from anytime soon. Her entire focus was on the list of cases, and whether there was anything related that might tie into the new theme they had identified.

An expansion on the flowers.

Perfume.

What did it signify? At this point she couldn't tell, but all she knew was that it widened their net for past events that might have a bearing on this case. And it was her job to review all of that, with Owen's help.

"Here it is," she said, as the record of the victims came up on their screen, and they studied the list together.

Yet again she was grateful that Owen was the fastest worker in terms of research. All he had to do was glance at the details, and his fingers literally flew over the keyboard.

She was sure that the records server at base literally smoldered when Owen started going in there. At least that briefly amusing thought distracted her in the microsecond before the first information flashed up.

"Aw, come on," Owen muttered.

"What is it?"

"Petunia Watson is the first victim to our knowledge. And I can find no trace of any trouble, or involvement with perfume or any other smell or chemical. And no record of any job at a department store or anywhere else that involved promoting perfume or dealing with it."

"Okay. Nothing on her, then," May said, looking sadly at their earliest name. "No wonder she didn't get into any trouble. She was only twenty when she died," she said regretfully.

"Maybe we should go for the older aged victims first?" Owen asked. "Not that any of these victims are old. I think the highest age I saw was about thirty-four. But the older ones could have had more opportunity for interactions and trouble and cases. Maybe some of them interacted with the killer, and others were targeted without them knowing about it. I mean, there are so many victims. Surely at least one of them knew him?"

"Let's do it that way," May said. They had to do it some way.

Owen clicked the mouse, pulling up the records for the thirty-four-year-old victim that was the oldest they had yet found.

"No, nothing for her so far. Going down, let's look at Tansy Toomey."

Again, Owen's fingers flashed over the screen so fast that May literally felt disoriented.

"Okay. Here's something."

The records flashed up and May leaned forward eagerly.

Tansy Toomey had been involved in a case, just a couple of months before her death.

"Assault," Owen muttered under his breath. His fingers accelerated over the keyboard once again as he called up the case details.

"Well!"

They both leaned forward and read the details of the assault case that Tansy had successfully won, with her attacker being given a fine and a suspended sentence.

"She was in a bar, and she was insulted by a man who criticized her saying that she was wearing perfume so strong it could set the whole place alight," May read aloud in a shocked voice. "He demanded that she move, and go elsewhere in the bar, because her scent was offensive to him."

"She retaliated, and refused to move, whereupon her attacker, Phil Jones, shoved her hard. This caused her to fall backward off her chair, and hit her head on the ground." Owen continued the story.

"Another customer in the bar tried to help Tansy, but Phil attacked him too, bruising him in several places and fracturing his wrist."

May's eyes widened. This was significant.

"This is so important," she said. "We can now place perfume, or specifically the mention of perfume, in the same room as a victim and the attacker of that victim. That's hugely significant."

"He was finally subdued by the manager and staff of the bar, who held him until the police arrived and took him away in handcuffs," Owen concluded.

"So the perfume connection suddenly makes sense," May said. "This was an attack on a woman in a bar, and which the assailant was criticizing her for using too much perfume. It strikes me as a very personal attack. It shows me that this man was triggered into violence by these scents. How old is this case?" She stared down at the date.

"It's eight years ago. So one of the earlier ones," Owen confirmed. "He could have killed before that, but it only became obvious at this point. And because it was a minor incident, he got away with it."

May looked again at the case report, which was aligning in many ways with the shadowy suspect she was seeking.

"Who is this man?" she asked. "Let's find more about who Phil Jones really is."

Owen went into another database, narrowing his eyes as he learned more about this aggressive attacker.

"He's a botanist!" he said in triumph, and May felt excitement flare inside her at this proof of a further connection with the interlinking evidence of flowers they were seeking.

"Where does he work?"

Owen's eyes widened. "Even more significant, May. He works at a nursery close to Chestnut Hill. By my estimation, it's a ten minute drive from the first site where we found the bodies."

That was it. May jumped up from her chair. Undoubtedly they had all the elements they needed to take this further. This suspect was triggered by perfume, he was violent, he targeted women, he worked with flowers, and he lived close to the biggest burial site they had yet discovered.

"We need to go and speak to him. Now," she said. "We need to ask him some important questions. Firstly, where he was on the day of the most recent killing. Did he have anything to do with Rosemary?"

She grabbed her purse from the back of the chair.

"Do we need to tell anyone?" Owen asked. "Should we notify the FBI?"

Considering that for a moment, as she looked at the activity surrounding them, May shook her head. "They're still too busy coordinating the search for burial sites. I think we would be distracting them if we came forward with this information, which is not a new development. It's just checking a detail."

"If he seems guilty, we can ask the FBI to join us for the questioning," Owen agreed.

May hoped that their trip would lead them straight to the guilty man. Threading their way through the frantic knots of FBI agents and police officers, she and Owen rushed out of the police department, and headed for the parking lot at a run.

CHAPTER NINETEEN

As they drove to Phil Jones's house, May concentrated on the road ahead, while Owen read more of the details on the case.

"It says here that Phil Jones had a history of negative and abusive comments toward women in the past. Old college associates had come forward to give testimony. They'd described him as aggressive, irrational, and prone to sudden violence."

"That's significant," May said.

"One of the old college classmates mentioned that he'd insulted her fragrance, saying it was stale and smelled of onions and she should avoid cheap perfumes."

May raised her eyebrows.

"So he is clearly very sensitive to smells, and also triggered by them."

Owen nodded.

May couldn't wait to get face to face with this man, even though she knew they would have to expect the unexpected when questioning a suspect who was unpredictable and could lash out at any given moment.

He could be violent toward her and Owen. Since they were going in without FBI backup, they had to take care. May just hoped they wouldn't get hurt in the process. But she was far too fired up to worry about that right now.

"I need to know exactly where he was when Rosemary was taken yesterday afternoon," she said.

They arrived at the nursery and pulled up outside. Immediately, May saw that this was a large and clearly thriving business. The location of the nursery was superb, right on a main street where it was possible to attract a lot of passing customers.

The large sign over the entrance was in the shape of a green tree, and the premises were large and imposing, set on at least ten acres of landscaped grounds. Areas of greenhouses could be seen at the front. There was a big board advertising their most popular indigenous plants, as well as the most sought after exotic flowers, trees, and shrubs. There looked to be a small café and also a kids' play area.

Clearly, Phil Jones was a man who could nurture growing things in the harshest environment, but did not have the same respect for humans.

She headed toward the main entrance, Owen following close behind. It was busy, at what May now saw was nine a.m. on a Sunday. Customers were thronging in. She hoped that on this popular day, Phil would be at work.

"How could a man who seems to dislike women and is so personally affected by them, work in a place like this?" Owen asked.

"I guess he's here working under orders, and is there only to care for the plants," May said. "But if we need to, we could ask the other staff if there have been any incidents between Phil and female customers."

Ahead, May saw a large reception counter, studded with pot plants and small shelves of seeds, gifts, plant food and other impulse purchases. May breathed in the scent of leaves and flowers, with an undertone of fertilizer. She guessed that someone obsessed with the aromas of petals and perfumes might find this a wholesome place.

Behind the greenery she could see two young and helpful looking attendants peering out. They both looked like college students, for whom this was a weekend gig.

"Morning," May said to the closest student, who had long hair and a goatee and was wearing a necklace with a crystal and a feather. "We're looking for Phil Jones."

"Phil. Where's Phil?" he asked the other, female attendant.

She scowled, seeming less pleased by the mention of his name, which May guessed was a clue.

"He's out back. I think he was attending to the water plants," she said. "If you go out the side entrance and follow the path around, you should find him."

May was about to leave, but then hesitated, wondering if she should ask something else that might be important.

"He works here full-time, right?" she asked.

"Well, yes. But he's not here all the time," the helpful man replied. "He's out of the nursery for much of the day, sourcing plants, going on field trips, and also planting at customers' houses." The woman added, "He doesn't deal with the public at all. If you need advice on plants, please ask one of our sales consultants, or you can also ask us here at the till."

"Thank you, but it's in connection with a police matter," May said. These red flags about Phil's nature were now showing up thick and fast.

She felt intrigued that right up front, they'd identified that this man had the flexibility to come and go as he needed to. He was not tied down to a nine to five on the premises, and that meant he would have had the opportunity to do what the killer had been doing.

Eagerly, May headed out of the nursery's main building and followed the path, as directed.

There was a small greenhouse on the right, which was densely planted with a variety of orchids. They walked around another shrubbery, planted in the shape of a peacock, featuring bright, colorful bushes, shrubs, and flowers.

It was a warm day, with a light breeze blowing, bringing in the aromas of the flowers and other vegetation. May breathed deeply, taking in the various scents, which seemed to be fighting one another for dominance.

Ahead, the buildings opened up into a green, sweeping lawn, lined with flower beds. On the far side was a small lake, about fifty yards wide, which was fed by a large ornate waterfall. In the center of the lake was an island with a tree, and a variety of water plants.

There was a small red boat moored next to the island, and on the island itself, she saw the man she guessed was their suspect.

He was dressed in jeans, a checked shirt, and designer sneakers. He had a short beard and slightly receding hair, and was crouched down, digging something from the side of the tree. She noticed that he seemed tall and burly, with muscular arms. Undoubtedly, he would have had the strength to kill and lift his female victims, if he was their killer.

Phil Jones didn't see her or Owen approach, as he was busy and absorbed in his task.

May looked around. They needed to get close to him. They couldn't exactly shout out questions across the expanse of blue-gray, glimmering water.

She saw a small, arched bridge to the left, which led across the lake and onto the island.

"Let's walk across and speak to him," she suggested to Owen.

She set off across the bridge, which had steel treads that clanged slightly as they walked.

The clanging alerted Phil and he looked up. May saw him clock them. He looked from one of them to the other. There was a considering expression in his eyes.

May decided that now she was more than halfway over the bridge, it was safe to engage in conversation with this suspect. He was now within earshot and could not pretend he couldn't hear.

"Phil Jones?" she called. "Deputy May Moore here. If you don't mind, we'd like to ask you a couple of questions."

Phil stood up. He stared at them for one more, frozen moment. And then, to May's alarm, he dropped his spade. He ran for the red boat and jumped into it. The boat rocked violently and water splashed up in a shimmering wave.

And then, Phil grabbed the oars and began rowing for all he was worth.

Rowing, May saw to her consternation, toward the back of the lake, where a narrow creek formed a waterway that led out of the nursery.

She couldn't quite believe that their suspect was attempting to make a water getaway, via a route of streams that might lead the whole way to Eagle Lake.

They needed to speak to him urgently, and had to stop this attempt at flight before he escaped the premises.

CHAPTER TWENTY

May raced across the footbridge, the metal treads clanging as she ran. Behind her, Owen was running, too, causing the flimsy structure to vibrate even more with his speed. May almost lost her balance as she ran, and had to make a grab for the equally flimsy rail to stop herself being bounced right off this bridge.

She reached the island. Her feet thudded down onto dry land. Somewhere on the other side, she heard the desperate splashing of Phil's oars against the water as he did his best to flee them via the river route out of the nursery.

She raced around the trees and bushes that provided cover in the island's center, following a paved path that snaked its way around the edge of the island, winding through burgeoning water plants, ornamental grasses, and a profusion of ferns.

May nearly lost her footing again, skidding on the paving stone and almost plowing into a large fern. It seemed everything here was slick, slippery, and covered with a fine but slimy layer of moisture and moss. But now she'd rounded the island and saw him in her sights.

He was rowing frantically as he headed for the outlet where this lake joined the main creek, and to her consternation, May saw that he was making good time. It looked as if the current was in his favor.

"Stop, please," she yelled. "We want to speak to you."

He rowed on, not pausing in his strokes, not reacting to her voice at all.

"Mr. Jones!" she shouted, but her voice was lost in the rushing of the water, and the gurgle of the waterfall, and the distant drone of a lawn mower some distance away. "Stop! We just want to talk to you!"

But he didn't stop. He rowed with grim determination, and May realized he was beginning to pull away from her.

She needed to stop him, before he got away. She glanced behind her. Owen had just rounded the corner of the island. She could see him pausing for a moment, looking around him, taking in his surroundings.

And then her deputy made his decision. With a gigantic splash, he leaped into the water.

It was deeper than May had thought. Just a couple of yards from the island, Owen was already up to his shoulders in the clear but cold looking water. Forging forward, he soon had to swim, powering after the fleeing botanist with a powerful crawl stroke.

He was nearing the boat! Owen was making headway. He was gaining on Phil, who was rowing even more frantically as the splashing deputy approached.

"Owen! Be careful!" May called.

She saw to her alarm that Phil had now abandoned the idea of flight. Instead, he was turning around in the boat and brandishing an oar angrily, clearly intending to fight Owen off.

The oar struck down, narrowly missing the deputy as he ducked underwater to avoid it. But then he managed to grab hold of the boat, as Phil raised the oar again. Aggression was written all over his face. May saw in his eyes that he wouldn't hesitate to hurt Owen, or worse.

She could hardly bear to watch as the botanist went on the attack. Owen looked so vulnerable there in the water, and the oars were heavy and long. Undoubtedly, if Phil got in a lucky blow, Owen would risk serious injury.

"Please, stop!" May shouted.

But neither Owen nor Phil seemed to hear her. She was too far away to intervene. And May knew she was nowhere near as fast a swimmer as her investigation partner was. She wouldn't get to them in time. By the time this was over, she'd still be splashing around near the island, trying to make headway. It would be better for her to stay where she was, so that if Owen did get hurt, she could call for immediate help.

Owen let go of the boat and plunged under the water as Phil brought down the oar. The heavy wooden blade slashed into the water, exactly where his head had been, and May drew in a horrified breath. The drag of the water would slow the oar - but not by that much. What if he hadn't gotten deep enough? Visions came to her of her deputy, with a serious head injury, drowning in the lake before she could reach him.

Where was he?

Phil lifted the oar again, scanning the lapping waters around the boat's stern, staring from side to side as he no doubt asked himself the same question.

"Owen!" May whispered.

He must have gotten hit. He could drown in seconds. May knew how to do CPR, but she'd have to get him to shore first, and did she even have enough time for that? Plus, she'd have to deal with the threat of Phil fighting her off, too - if he hadn't already made his escape. And if he had, she would not only have a badly hurt deputy, but they would have lost their chances at capturing a suspect.

May hesitated, adrenaline surging as she finalized her plan of action.

And then, just as she took a deep breath, preparing to dive into the waters to save her deputy, Owen surfaced.

But he didn't come up at the boat's stern, where he'd gone under. He erupted from the water on the far side of the boat, at its prow. Phil now had his back to him, glaring down at the lapping waters as he clutched his oar.

Owen grabbed hold of the side of the boat and bore down on it with all his weight. The boat rocked violently, and with a yell, Phil pinwheeled his arms, letting go of the oar as he fought for balance.

But it was a losing fight, and Owen had the critical element of surprise on his side. A moment later, the botanist toppled into the lake, landing with a massive splash that sent water fountaining into the air.

"Owen! You did it!" May yelled. She felt a sense of triumph and awe at the flawless way that her deputy had executed this clever strategy.

Phil was flailing in the water, clearly a stronger rower than swimmer. Ducking under again, Owen surfaced, with a firm hold on one of the man's ankles. Now yelling and spluttering, Phil had no choice but to fight to keep his head above water, thrashing his arms and coughing as Owen towed him back to shore.

May ran to meet them, reaching Owen as he dragged Phil back to the island. He was coughing and cussing, and his face was red with effort. And then, with a heave and a mighty splash, Owen hauled him out of the water.

Phil sat there for a moment, shivering and coughing, clearly unimpressed with the pair of them.

"On your feet!" May commanded. "Put your hands on your head, and get on your feet."

Glowering at her, he scrambled to his feet, slipping on one of the water ferns before regaining his balance.

"What is this all about? Why were you chasing me?" he complained aggressively.

"Why did you run?" May countered.

Seeing that his teeth were now chattering in the brisk breeze that was fluttering the grasses, and knowing that Owen must also be freezing after his dunking in the glassy lake, May decided that they needed to regroup before the questioning.

"Come with us. We're going to take you inside where it's dry. And then, we need you to answer our questions."

"I don't know what you mean. I haven't done anything wrong."

"I think you do," May said.

"Wha - What is this all about?" he repeated.

"We'll tell you - but not until we're inside."

The botanist now looked worried, rather than aggressive.

May didn't trust him, and thought he would still try to make another break for freedom if he got the chance.

Grasping an arm each, firmly, they led him across the bridge and back to the nursery, where May hoped they would learn the truth about why this man had acted so guiltily when he saw the police arrive.

CHAPTER TWENTY ONE

Fifteen minutes later, May had set up a room to the side of the nursery's main offices. The manageress on duty had been able to procure one of the nursery's staff jackets. Phil was wrapped in it, while Owen was wearing his own jacket, which he'd left in the back of May's car as the day had warmed.

A heater was glowing in the middle of the room. Steaming gently as they stood close to it, May saw that Phil and Owen were still glaring at each other suspiciously. Clearly, her deputy didn't trust Phil an inch - and why should he, May thought, after the botanist had attempted to do him serious harm with that oar?

"Now, Mr. Jones, we need to ask you some questions," May said.

"I don't have to answer you," Phil shot back.

"You are under no obligation to do so. But before you decide whether or not to answer, I must inform you that you have already committed a serious felony. You assaulted an officer of the law, and it is only thanks to his quick thinking and reactions that he wasn't seriously hurt, or even killed." May stared inexorably at the shivering Phil, hoping that she was getting the message across to him. She needed him to understand that he was already in trouble.

"If you cooperate with us, it will reflect better on you now," May said in stern tones.

"I - look, I didn't know you were police!" he said. "I was just - just going for a row while I was on my tea break."

May folded her arms. She wasn't going to accept this evasive answer.

"You abandoned your duties on the island and leaped into the boat when we called you by your name. I also announced that we were police," May pressed on.

"I didn't hear you. I'm hard of hearing, especially when I'm out on the water."

May decided to stop arguing semantics. It was more important to cut straight to the point of why they were here, and find out what Phil's association with the victims was.

"You had charges laid against you a few years ago for assaulting a woman who was later found murdered," May said. "I'm talking about Tansy Toomey."

Phil pressed his lips together. May noted he now seemed unsure.

"That's nonsense. I never killed anyone. I didn't kill Tansy."

"You assaulted her and said you found her perfume offensive. Then, just a couple of months later, she disappeared. We recently found her body in one of the mass graves we are unearthing," May explained.

"I don't know anything about that," Phil insisted.

"We believe you might know a lot more than you're telling us," May said.

"I know nothing! I never even assaulted her. Those charges were trumped up. The jury was biased."

He was now tense and trembling, despite standing close to the heater. The man was clearly lying, but she needed to pin him down, and find out what he was hiding.

"We think you do know more. And since several other women were buried in the same place, we need you to answer our questions."

Phil was shaking his head in disbelief. "That's not true. You have to be able to prove that. You can't just accuse me of things like this," he blustered.

"Our investigation is still ongoing. And the more you try to lie to us, the worse it will look for you," May said. "You probably think that we are going to accuse you of all of these murders. However, I assure you, there is a way out of this for you if you simply answer our questions truthfully and honestly."

Phil shrugged defiantly.

May decided that they weren't going to get any more answers here. Now that he was dry enough, they needed to move to a more formal setting, and question him in one of the interview rooms at the police department. This would mean that Kerry would also be involved, and May felt happy about that. Her sister was a very effective questioner, and right now, she would be pissed and aggressive, more than a match for Phil.

The fact he was being so evasive and obstructive was speaking volumes for his guilt, May thought. And since they were now here on the premises, she decided that it would be a good idea to take a look in his car.

She wanted to see if there was anything in it that he could have used as a murder weapon.

"Please can you hand me your car keys," she asked him.

"My car keys? Why?"

Now he didn't just look defiant. He looked anxious, too, as if he was worried about showing them what was in his car. And that made May even more eager to know what it was that he wanted to hide.

She was not going to relent. She wanted to explore every angle.

"Yes. You have to. Please take us to your vehicle and unlock it, to show us the interior. Once we've had a look, we'll take you to the police department for questioning."

"I'm an innocent man," he muttered, the aggression back in his voice.

"If you are, all you have to do is prove it to us," May countered reasonably.

Phil looked deeply reluctant as he trailed out of the small side room and over to one of the staff lockers that were situated near the nursery's entrance.

May and Owen followed him, Owen's feet still squelching in his shoes.

Phil unlocked the locker and took out his car keys. Then, also squelching, he walked out of the nursery. Owen walked closely beside him and May followed behind. They were both alert and ready in case this man tried to make a break for it again.

Phil led them to a Suzuki SUV parked in the shade of a tree. May regarded the car with interest, deciding that he could very easily have fitted the victims inside this vehicle, which was spacious enough to accommodate a body either in the back seat or else the trunk.

Phil unlocked the car and opened the driver's door.

May took a quick look inside. She blinked in surprise at what she saw. Then she felt her heart speed up.

Scattered on the front seat of the car were about five perfume samples. May could smell their intermingled scent emanating from the fabric seat cover.

The samples sported the logo of the department store where Rosemary had done the promotions. Things were adding up. She was starting to see how the trail of evidence was pointing back in this suspect's direction.

She glanced into the back seat, and there, she saw something else that added to the compelling story.

There was a long, heavy looking walking stick on the back seat. Its base looked to be dark with mud and soil – or perhaps it was not just soil, but something else as well.

May turned to Owen.

"Take a look in there," she said in a low voice, keeping a firm hold on Phil's arm.

Based on the contents of his car which she'd seen at a glance, May knew this suspect had gotten even stronger. In fact, she felt certain that they were now onto something important.

It was time to bring him, and get the FBI, and particularly Kerry, to question this man further.

If he was the killer, they needed to get the full story from him, and Kerry was the woman best able to do that.

May was willing to hand over that important step at this point. The entire county was in a state of panic, and if the evidence pointed to a suspect, May knew that she had to put her own ego aside, and do whatever it took to get the truth from him.

CHAPTER TWENTY TWO

May paced away from the botanist's car, quickly making the call she needed to Sheriff Jack, who she knew was at the Fairshore police department. She hoped that this would be the best way to get the FBI's full resources on board with the search and interrogation.

Excitement filled her that they might be bringing in the killer at last.

Sheriff Jack answered. "May, I saw you head out earlier after looking at the cases. I'm guessing you went after a lead?"

She felt pleased that Sheriff Jack had guessed so accurately.

"Yes, I did. We have a strong lead, Phil Jones. He's a botanist who works at the Chestnut Hill nursery, with a record of violence. He had charges laid against him a few years back, after abusing one of the earlier victims, Tansy Toomey."

"That's significant," Jack said.

"He fled when he saw us arrive to question him. He's refusing to cooperate with the questioning, but there's some important evidence in his car, including perfume samples from the department store where Rosemary worked, as well as a heavy stick," May said quietly. "I think we need to get the FBI's forensic examiners involved here, and bring him in for further questioning."

"Perfume samples? That would link up with what we've discovered so far," Jack said thoughtfully. "And any potential weapon should be analyzed if it aligns with the M.O. I'm going to send the FBI forensics crew there as soon as possible. Your sister Kerry arrived at the police department about an hour ago. She brought in a possible suspect who lived in the neighborhood near the gravesite, but he's just been cleared. So she's waiting here."

"I'd like Kerry to question him," May said firmly.

"I'll tell her you're on your way, and that she must stand by. And I'll brief her on the case so far. Well done, May. That was some good work there. We have a strong suspect. Let's hope that between the evidence and the questioning, he's proven to be the killer," Jack said.

*

Twenty minutes later, May pulled up outside the Fairshore police department. All the parking spots were full, and cars were parked the whole way down the road. She stopped outside the police department and let Owen and Phil out of the car. From inside, she saw Sheriff Jack rush out to meet them.

Then May drove back down the road to find a place to park. It seemed that everyone had converged here. She spotted a TV van, several police cars from other departments, two vehicles that, from their sleek and dark appearance she imagined must belong to the FBI, and a host of other cars belonging to ordinary people in the town.

Right at the end of the road, May was able to squeeze into a spot on the sidewalk. Climbing out, she quickly jogged back to the police department. At the door, she saw that her sister, Kerry, was waiting.

Kerry, with her arms folded, was staring around the area with an authoritarian gaze. May immediately noticed the lack of a ring on her engagement finger.

"Hi, sis," Kerry said. "Good work for bringing in this suspect. They're getting him ready for me now, and will call me when the room's set up."

"Hey, Kerry. I'm sorry about what's happened." May felt it was better to mention the broken engagement immediately. She felt a surprising rush of sympathy for her sister. The break-up must have been traumatic for her, and now she was having to return to a town where every different street probably reminded her of one or another of her wedding plans.

Kerry saw the direction of May's gaze immediately.

"He never got the ring back when I threw it out," she said.

"Oh!" May's eyes widened.

"Brandon seemed quite angry about that. He was shouting that it had been expensive. I said I didn't care, and he should have thought of that before he did what he did. He almost threw himself out after it," Kerry remembered. "Pity he didn't."

"I agree," May said loyally.

"Last I saw, it was picked up by a homeless man. Hopefully he sold it and got himself a few good meals. Brandon didn't get downstairs in time to save it. I don't even think he got much of his underwear back, but at least people were laughing at him for that," she remembered in a bitter voice.

"I hope so. I'm so sorry it didn't work out," May said.

Kerry shrugged irritably. May remembered she was never at her best when something went wrong in her life. She could see she was seething, and ready to take her anger out on the closest person. Everyone walked on eggshells when Kerry was mad, May remembered.

"Well, perhaps we should stop discussing my personal life," she snapped. "That's not why I'm here. I'm sorry that we appear to have a killer like this who's terrorizing the area."

"I know. I can't believe these mass graves," May said sadly.

"They've discovered more bodies in that third site you pinpointed. There are about four more buried there."

"That's horrific." May felt shocked to her core. This monster was one of the worst serial killers she'd ever heard of. She simply could not comprehend the magnitude of his crimes, the loss of so many innocent lives. Chills prickled her spine almost painfully.

Kerry clearly felt the same, shaking her head angrily.

"To think that one of the most murderous criminals in history has been active in our own county! When we were teenagers, this guy was taking women and killing them. And he's still doing it. Do you think he got Lauren?" Kerry sounded worried. "That's been on my mind ever since I heard how long he's been active for."

"I thought of that immediately, too. I feel sick every time I think of those bodies getting dug up. But the one thing we do know is that so far, every one of his victims has a flower name."

"True."

"And Lauren doesn't."

"So what?"

"So I don't know if he would have targeted her."

"What if he made a mistake?" Kerry glowered at her. "That could have happened. It would be stupid not to think that."

Now Kerry was calling her stupid. May felt her hackles rise, and subdued her irritation with an effort. Kerry was very upset. She was in a terrible mood. And they could not afford to do anything but cooperate with such an important case to solve.

"He hasn't made any mistakes yet. He's been very, very careful. You don't get to remain active for over ten years in a small community by making mistakes. But perhaps when you question him, you'll find out more. I just hope you can get him to tell us more, or even confess."

May found herself hoping with all her heart that Kerry's bad mood might break through the shell of resistance that Phil was presenting her with.

Even though she felt utterly riled by her sister's nasty behavior, May had to admit that if anyone could get the truth from her suspect, it was her sister in this current mood. May was not sure that she would have been successful in a similar situation.

At that moment, there were footsteps from behind, and May saw Kerry's investigation partner, the tall, preppy-looking Adams, hurry out.

"Morning, Adams," she greeted him politely.

"Morning, May," he said absently, as if she wasn't important enough for a fully enthusiastic greeting. "Kerry, the room's ready. The suspect is set up. We had a short struggle with him, so we've handcuffed him. Shall we question him together?"

Kerry nodded at Adams, looking satisfied. "Let's do just that," she said.

May decided she was going to go and watch from the observation room.

For once, she wouldn't feel jealous at all if Kerry managed to get the breakthrough that May was sure was waiting ahead.

She couldn't wait to see an angry Kerry let loose on her uncooperative suspect. May hoped that her furious sister was going to be able to force the truth from this violent and secretive man.

CHAPTER TWENTY THREE

With bated breath, May watched from the observation room at the Fairshore police department, as Kerry marched inside, with Adams close behind, ready to confront Phil Jones.

May felt overwhelmingly anxious that this case should be solved, and the killer caught. She'd done her part and now it was up to the FBI to take it further.

With Kerry in her worst mood ever, doing the interrogation, May felt confident that they had the best possible person in place to get results.

She thought that it was a ninety percent certainty that they were right about him. The evidence would corroborate his guilt, hopefully. Finding a weapon was an important step. More important would be finding traces of blood and DNA on the edge of that stick, or in the car. And equally important would be the in-person testimony from the interrogation.

Owen huddled beside her, peering through the window.

"I wonder how she'll handle this," he whispered.

"Aggressively, I suspect," May whispered back.

Kerry looked as pissed as May had ever seen her, as she faced up to Phil Jones.

"Mr. Jones," she said firmly. "I'm FBI Agent Moore and I'm here to question you."

"Yes, officer?" Phil snapped, leaning back in his chair. He, too, looked pissed, resentful, and uncooperative. He was most definitely an antisocial person, May thought. He almost didn't seem to be able to cope around people.

May saw Kerry look briefly annoyed that she had been addressed as officer after she had specifically told him she was an FBI agent. Kerry was picky like that, and more so when she was angry for other reasons.

"You know why you're here," Kerry said, glowering at him as she sat down.

"I'm here because you're falsely accusing me," he retorted.

"Well, certain evidence has been brought to light," Kerry said. "Evidence that points to your involvement in some of the murders that have been taking place in this county."

He stared at her, sullenly uncooperative, as she continued.

"When our local law enforcement approached you to ascertain more facts, you chose to run. To run! Not exactly the actions of an innocent man, I am sure you will agree. And you subsequently attacked deputy Lovell with an oar."

"He pushed me out of the boat!" Phil argued.

"You attacked him first," Kerry insisted.

"Because I was scared," Phil replied, his voice quavering.

"That we'd find out what you'd done?"

"No, no. I'm scared of the police in general. I don't like people. Only plants."

"Explain yourself?" Kerry challenged him. There was something in her eye that clearly triggered Phil enough for words to burst out of him.

"I'm not a people person. I'm a plant person. I don't talk to any of the customers. You ask the manager. I'm only allowed to work in areas when the customers are not there. Everyone knows, I'm good with plants but not with people."

May knew that his words were confirming what she'd already guessed - that they were dealing with a highly antisocial man here, who was not by any means normal in his interactions.

And that added to his potential guilt because the killer was surely not a normal person.

"Did you know Rosemary Pharr?" Kerry asked.

"Rosemary?" Was that a flash of recognition in his eyes, May wondered. "No, I never knew her."

"Did you ever visit the mall where she worked?"

"No. Why are you asking me these questions?"

"Because you had perfume samples from that department store in your car. If you didn't visit the mall, how did you get them? She was handing them out, the afternoon before she died."

There was a short silence in the room. Phil now looked pale.

"Where were you yesterday afternoon?" Adams asked. "Can you account for your movements?"

"I - I was out and about. I had a few things to do. Some plants to buy. I was driving around."

"Do you have a record of where and when you stopped off?" Kerry said.

"I don't have the times. I can - I can tell you where I went. I – I might have gone past the mall." Now he was looking hunted.

May felt a surge of triumph at this small, but surely significant admission. Bit by bit, she was sure, Kerry would erode this man's defenses.

Kerry tapped her fingers on the desk. "If you like plants so much and not people, how did you end up with a stack of perfume samples in the back of your car? Because clearly you didn't get those from a plant. You got them from a person. Do you remember which person?" She stared at him closely.

Phil swallowed. "I don't remember."

"You expect me to believe that you don't remember where you got a wad of perfume samples from?" Kerry asked, her voice dripping with scorn.

"There are - there are certain smells I like," he explained. "I like to surround myself with those smells. I collect samples. You see, I hate cheap perfumes. The smells trigger me and I end up losing my temper. It calms me to be around perfumes that smell good, that have that – like – that quality blend of aromatics."

May felt extremely impressed that Kerry was getting Phil to talk so much. He was opening up under her relentless interrogation, and revealing personal details and complexities. She hoped it wouldn't be long before Kerry got to the truth. Losing his temper over smells felt like a significant admission.

"So that's why you take samples?"

"Yes. I was looking to take some home. You see, there are some perfumes that I can't afford because they're too expensive. Really expensive."

"Is that so?"

"Yes. That's so. I have – I have mood problems, I know I do. I use it in the house. On the couch, on my pillow. Perfume stabilizes my mood, but I can't afford it. I mean, you think I'm a bad person. But I work hard for a low wage. I work six days a week, eleven hours a day. Long hours. You can look at my bank statements. My car costs money, and gas, because I live out of town. And I donate to a dog shelter. I'm not bad. But this woman was handing out samples, and I saw that there were a few of the ones I like. The really good ones. So I took them. She let me have a few. I don't even remember the woman who gave them to me. I wasn't interested in her at all. I dot the perfumes around the house. The samples are tiny, they don't go far, but that's what I do."

May blinked. Kerry sure had gotten this witness to say a lot. Okay, so not much of it was relevant, but at least he was talking.

Kerry didn't even seem to be listening. She'd linked her hands behind her head, and although May couldn't see her face, she was sure her sister was rolling her eyes.

"You seem to have a lot of time available for talking," she said in a hard voice. "I, however, don't. I need to get information from you. And so far, it has not been forthcoming. So let's try another angle. Your movements yesterday. Tell me about them. I need to know where you were, and when."

As Kerry spoke, May had a strange sensation, a flash of insight in her mind, nothing more than a flicker.

Was she missing something, she wondered. What had just happened there? She felt as if her brain was trying to tell her something, but she wasn't quite able to pick up the message.

"You don't believe me. But I can tell you now. I have a good nose. I can pick up some perfumes, not all. I can tell right now you're wearing Chanel no. 5. It's a very nice perfume. Quality."

Kerry raised her eyebrows, looking more impressed than May thought she wanted to.

"Your partner here, I think he's wearing Brut deodorant."

Adams recoiled, looking shocked.

"You see, I know my scents. I know my smells. But I don't know enough. There are people at the perfume counter with better noses than me, and they can literally tell you what any perfume is. But I know what I need to. Bad perfume offends me. And I might have spent more time at the mall than I should, because I was trying to get more samples. But I can't tell you that for sure. Because it could get me into trouble with work."

Again, May had that stab of insight and again, she missed it. She gasped, as it came and went, too fast for her to get it.

Owen turned to her, looking concerned. "You okay? Leg cramping?" he asked.

"No," May explained. "My brain keeps prodding me, but every time I try to think why, I don't get it."

Owen nodded. "I hate when that happens. There must be a reason. Do you think it was something that was being said in the interrogation? Not that there's been much said," he added doubtfully.

"It must have sparked my thoughts."

"Was it about the mall?" Owen questioned. "About the samples?"

And then, May got it. She breathed out with a big, worried sigh.

"It's the perfume. Owen, Rosemary was doused in it. I mean, it was really, really strong. And very distinctive."

"Yes. To smell it so strongly, he must have done that," Owen said.

"I was so sure about this suspect, Phil Jones, but suddenly I'm not so sure anymore, because I'm thinking he really can't afford perfume. He begs for samples, but the samples are so tiny that he could not have drenched the victims' clothing with perfume in the way we've been seeing. That was probably a whole bottle poured onto the jacket, to saturate it that way and cause such a big stain."

"Definitely not a sample size," Owen agreed.

"And he lives far out of town, and works long hours. How would he stalk his victims so effectively? I am starting to feel something is wrong here, that the killer is someone who has more time to plan. And more money."

"You could be right," Owen agreed. He sounded reluctant to be stepping away from this strong suspect, but May thought he saw her point. "You could be right. But all that means so far is that instead of one suspect, we have none again. How can we get more information on who he is?"

May's mind raced ahead, thinking about what she'd just learned about perfumes, and the people who had good noses and were able to identify them.

"What if the perfume is this killer's signature?" May suggested, as her brain finally pieced together the faint pattern she was starting to see. "What if he hasn't used it on just one victim, but on all of them? And what if it's the same perfume? It smelled so distinctive. Perhaps it has significance for him. Perhaps it smells strongly of flowers, or something else that draws him to it. Surely there must be a chance that if this theory is right, and we can learn more about the perfume, it might help us identify him? I mean, we have the time right now. We're not doing anything else. We could at least explore the idea, while Kerry is busy."

She stared at him, feeling anxious about what he might say.

"Yes," Owen said. "I do think it's worth it. That guy was accurate, and if we know the perfume, it might get us further. If we go and speak to Andy Baker, we might be able to find out if it's been used on other victims, and whether it's his signature. And then we can see if there's a way to identify it."

CHAPTER TWENTY FOUR

May hurried through to the back office, where Sheriff Jack was still busy speaking to two of the FBI. He turned as soon as he saw her approach.

"Jack, we've had an idea. It involves perfume, and the killer's possible use of it as a signature. Could we follow it up? I know we've got a seemingly strong suspect in custody but there are details that are making me unsure," May said.

Jack nodded. "You go right ahead. Whatever we can do, whatever leads we can follow, we must. If you feel unsure, there's a reason for it. Just keep me in the loop, May. I have media literally camping on our doorstep."

May could see that was true. Because when she went out of the police department, she and Owen had to walk all the way down the road to reach her car. May got three photographs taken along the way, even though she turned her head toward Owen as they passed.

At least the walk gave them a chance to do some breathless planning.

"How are we going to work this?" May asked.

"We need to go to the pathologists' offices, and we need to ask Andy Baker if we can identify any other traces of perfume from the earlier bodies," May said.

It was creepy in the extreme. She didn't know if it would even be possible. But Owen seemed to have embraced her theory.

"That perfume smell was really, really strong. It has to mean something."

"Really?" May said, impressed by his insight at such a time.

"Yes. It flashed across my mind. But then, with everything else that was happening, it flashed right out again. Same as happened with you, I guess."

"So we definitely need to explore that, then. Let's see if it gets us anywhere," May said, climbing into the car. "I guess that the next most recent body, Lily Gregory, would be the one we need to look at first. He killed her two weeks ago. Perhaps Andy can find some traces or signs of perfume on her clothing. If so, we know we're right, and then we have to see if we can figure out what it is."

"I have a feeling it might get us somewhere, faster than Kerry is going to get," Owen said wryly as he got in the passenger side.

May and Owen sped to the pathologists' office, and as they drove, May felt determined that this trip would lead to answers, and that they would be able to get what they needed from Andy Baker and his team. The more she thought about it, the more convinced she was that perfume, and perhaps one specific perfume, played a role in the killings.

It was part of the ritual or part of his signature. And it might give them the break they needed to trace this cunning and elusive man.

*

Twenty minutes later, May parked the car outside the forensic offices, and they both climbed hurriedly out. The morning was bathed in sunshine. From far away across the valley, she heard church bells ringing. It was a normal, everyday Sunday - except it wasn't, because they were on a hunt for the most important clue yet. The one that might lead them to the killer.

With her own fragile theory, Andy Baker's expertise, and the power of the FBI to help them, she hoped it would be possible.

May hurried into the building.

She wasn't surprised to see that it was a hive of activity, busier than she'd ever seen it. She recognized a couple of the local forensics experts, and saw a few others whose faces she didn't know at all, and who must be a part of the FBI contingent.

She walked up to the reception desk. The receptionist looked harassed with all this activity as she turned to May and Owen.

"Morning, deputies. How can I help you?" she asked.

"Is Andy Baker available?" May said.

"He's in laboratory five, examining one of the older remains with the FBI," the receptionist told her solemnly, her usually good natured face creased in a frown.

"Could you call him?"

"Sure," she said, sounding apologetic, as if the stress of the situation and all the people around, had made her forget her job for a moment. She picked up the phone and dialed.

"Is Dr. Baker in there? Deputy Moore and Lovell are here to see him." She replaced the phone. "He'll be with you now," she said.

May waited, listening to the murmur of voices and the trill of phones, the tread of feet and the distinctive noise of gurneys being wheeled into the postmortem rooms.

And then, from the bustling rooms beyond, Andy Baker hurried out. He was dressed in PPE, with a mask on, and had clearly come straight from an examination. His eyebrows raised when he saw them there.

"May, Owen. How can I help?"

May stepped forward. Suddenly, at this critical moment, nerves surged inside her. This was so desperately important. What if they didn't get what they needed? What if they couldn't? They needed a tangible link before they pursued this theory further, otherwise it would be no more than a useless dead end. They had to know if they were taking the right path, with this creative and unusual line of thinking.

"We need to find something from Lily Gregory's remains," she said. "Do you know if we would be able to examine her clothing? We think the killer might be using perfume as a signature, pouring it onto the victims before he kills them. We need to confirm that theory and then, if it's correct, we need to try and work out which perfume it is."

Now Andy's brows rose even higher.

"A scent used as a signature?" he asked, sounding surprised.

May nodded, feeling unsure all over again.

"Let's go and have a look. Her clothing has all been removed and itemized, and it's in plastic, in the refrigerated storage. We can take it out and see. With the older bodies, as you know, we usually apply something on our mask while we work, to make the smell bearable. Eucalyptus oil is my product of choice. But it does mean I wouldn't have picked up a hint of perfume when I packed the clothing away."

Quickly, May and Owen tugged on the gloves and head covers they needed to ensure that this sterile environment was not contaminated. May quickly put foot covers over her shoes.

They then followed Andy Baker down the passage, far along it, all the way to the end, where a white-painted door that led to the storage room, was firmly closed. Andy swiped a card to open it.

The lock buzzed, and clicked open. He swung the door wide and walked inside. May followed him, and Owen walked in and closed the door again.

They were in an enormous, brightly lit room that was very cold. May guessed that when storing clothing and possessions that had been on a corpse, cold was needed. Her breath steamed in the air and her skin prickled into goose bumps.

Andy's feet sounded loud in the silent room as he trod across the polished floor, looking at the labeled steel doors of the evidence lockers.

"Here we are," he said. He pulled open a drawer. Inside was a plastic bag, which had garments in it, neatly labeled.

May knew this would be a testing job. Carrying the bag over to a steel table, Andy unfolded the garments carefully.

"Here's the top she was wearing," he said. He placed a lacy mauve garment on the steel. "Here is her underwear. And she was wearing jeans and a light jacket."

Carefully and with the respect that May knew he would show, he placed the clothing in a row.

May glanced at Owen. This was their chance, to prove or disprove what they thought might take them further.

"So you say we're looking for any trace of a scent."

Andy peered down at the lilac blouse and then looked at the lapels of the fabric jacket.

"You know, what I am seeing here, is an oily stain. It's very faint but it's discernible. Take a look. It's on the fabric of the blouse and also on the jacket."

"Could it be perfume residue?" May asked.

"Looks like it could. There are a lot of things it could be. But an expensive, concentrated perfume will have a lot of oils in it and it might well leave a light stain. That's why they always say you should be careful about spraying perfume directly onto clothing, as it can stain."

May guessed that if perfume had caused the stain, there was surely a chance that some residue of the scent itself might remain.

"Here, on the lapels. This is where I'm seeing the mark the most."

Andy bent forward, holding his mask away from his face. He remained by the clothing for a minute. Then he straightened up, looking surprised.

"What do you think?" he asked.

May bent forward.

She inhaled carefully, picking up a medley of different scents. An undertone of rot that made her stomach twist. A hint of earth.

And above and beyond those, she caught the distinctive fragrance that she remembered breathing in from Rosemary's corpse, that she'd seen in that flowery graveyard.

"It's there! Definitely!"

Owen bent forward and breathed in.

"May, it's the same," he said. "Undoubtedly the same. This woman was doused in this perfume when she was killed. No way would she have applied it so that it stained the whole of her clothing. He's using it. For sure. And now, we need to find out what it is. Perhaps he's even buying it up from the department store in town."

May saw the excitement in his eyes as he stared at her.

For the first time in this case, they had a strong and solid lead, a direct connection that they could follow, and if they did, it might just lead them to the killer.

CHAPTER TWENTY FIVE

Half an hour later, May pulled up outside the mall where, just yesterday, Rosemary Pharr had been so brutally snatched.

They were here to ask what was surely the strangest and most macabre favor that the department store had encountered in a long while.

"I hope someone there is willing to do this. And I hope that Phil Jones was right about the accuracy of their noses," May said.

They climbed out of the car.

May took the plastic bag that Andy Baker had released to them. After consulting together with him on the best way forward, Andy had agreed to let them snip a piece of Rosemary Pharr's jacket from the store of clothing in the evidence bag. This was his most recent kill, still drenched in scent.

They had cut a small piece of fabric away from the jacket, where the distinctive perfume smell was the strongest. That was now safely inside this plastic packet.

Together, they marched into the mall and headed down the corridor.

May felt as if this innocent trip into a shopping emporium was somehow going to be a make or break moment in the case.

The more May thought about this case, the more she became convinced that Phil Jones was not their killer, and there was somebody lurking in the shadows. Somebody who was far too clever and experienced to be caught with a potential murder weapon in their car.

Somebody who had been operating silently, lethally, for more than ten years in their quiet town.

That somebody wasn't going to reveal themselves to May's team, she was sure of it. They had to find him. And so far, they didn't have much to go on. But perhaps this visit would open their eyes.

And then, May truly believed they might be able to start nailing down their killer.

At this hour, the mall was busy. It was full of Sunday morning shoppers, strolling around with no sense of urgency at all. Feeling stressed, May wove her way through the loitering shoppers, heading for the brightly lit entrance to the department store.

May glanced inside. She could see that, as she'd expected, there were security cameras everywhere. If the killer had come here to buy his perfume, perhaps that would be a way of tracking him.

Although, what if he'd even been too clever for that?

"Let's go in and check this out," she said to Owen.

They walked inside, and immediately May heard the pleasant music and smelled the mingled scents that were designed to draw in customers, to lure them into this sumptuous space and make them linger while they shopped.

With no intention of lingering, May headed for the perfume counter.

A white-uniformed attendant with dark hair and a red-lipstick smile hurried over.

"How can I help?" she asked.

"We are police officers investigating the recent murders," May said, and saw the woman instantly pale.

"We heard about Rosemary. It's too terrible. We can't believe she's gone. We were saying this morning, the girls and I, that anything we can do to help, we will."

"Is anyone in your team an expert at identifying perfume scents?" May asked.

Immediately, the attendant nodded. "Josh is the manager of the fragrances and cosmetics section. He has, like, a unique ability to identify perfumes. He even does work for some of the perfume houses."

"Is Josh here?"

The attendant checked her watch. "Yes, he should be. He was going to drive through to our other branch, but he shouldn't have left yet. Let me call him."

Quickly, she took out her phone and dialed. She spoke briefly.

"He's coming right now," she said.

Now, she looked curious, as if wondering why Josh's skill was needed by the police.

A few moments later, a dark haired and smartly dressed man hurried over. He was slim, in his mid-twenties, and immaculately groomed, with a helpful smile on his face.

"Morning, morning. How can I help?" he asked. Then his eyes widened as he took in who they were. "This is police business? Is anyone here a suspect?" he asked anxiously. May could see he was deeply worried that one of his team might have been Rosemary's killer.

"At this stage we are gathering evidence," May explained. "And we desperately need your help. We need you to identify a scent, if you can, from this piece of fabric."

She held up the plastic bag.

"Sure, I can do that," Josh said confidently. But May wasn't done yet. She needed to warn this man what the implications were.

"Before you go ahead, I must inform you that this fabric is from Rosemary's jacket. When her body was found early this morning, it was clear that the fabric had been doused in strong and very distinctive smelling perfume. The killer must have done it, and that's why we are here."

Now Josh looked utterly shocked. May hoped he wasn't too put off by the macabre nature of the request to agree to the favor.

"Doused in perfume? But she doesn't wear it! She's allergic!" he exclaimed. "That's one of the reasons I hesitated to hire her, although she turned out to be a fabulous salesperson. But yes, she wouldn't have done that. So he did it? That's totally weird. I'm a little unsettled by it, I must admit." He paused, and May could see he was totally creeped out by having to do this particular task. But then Josh pulled himself together.

"Give me the fabric, please," he said. "I'll see if I can identify this scent."

"Thank you," May said, meaning each heartfelt word.

With hands that shook slightly, the perfumery manager drew the piece of turquoise fabric out of the plastic bag. He sniffed it, at first hesitantly, and then more deeply.

"Now this is interesting. Very interesting," he said.

"Can you tell what it is?" May asked, anxiety flaring. Would he be able to provide the help they so desperately needed?

"I can tell you what this perfume is. But it's one that we don't stock anymore," the manager said, with a frown. "We haven't brought in stock for years, although I do think we still have a tester somewhere in the back. It's extremely expensive. One of the most expensive scents there is – or rather, was."

"Was?" May said.

"Yes, was. The perfume is called Joy, by Jean Patou. One of the finest fragrances ever made. It's been on the market for decades. It's extremely deep, extremely rich. Its signature notes are rose and jasmine. For many years it's been produced in extremely limited quantities, hence its astronomical price. But a couple of years ago, I believe the company was bought out, and they made the decision to discontinue it. Now there is a new perfume called Joy, produced by Dior, but it has a very different fragrance, which is more sandalwood based. Let me see if we have the old tester bottle for Joy by Jean Patou, here." He turned and rummaged in a cupboard behind the counter.

May felt stunned by the information she'd received.

Finally, they had a very clear lead that could give them a far better insight into the killer.

He used a distinctive perfume that was extremely expensive and had a very intense signature scent.

But that perfume had been recently discontinued. Now, May thought she knew why his killing interval was speeding up. Perhaps he was panicking. Perhaps the anticipated shortage, and eventual lack, of the scent he used was making him hurry, and causing him to make errors in his haste.

And perhaps, because of the shortage, he was buying up what he could. Stockpiling.

This information was pure gold.

They had a better chance now of finding this man, May knew it. This exotic, expensive perfume might just be the key that led them to him.

CHAPTER TWENTY SIX

The hunter felt his heart accelerate, feeling uncharacteristically anxious as he drove slowly past the place where his prey lived, wondering if she would be home, and if he could try again.

Last night, it had not been possible to take her, although he'd wanted to. When he saw her waiting for her cab, he had been convinced that the time was right.

But it hadn't been. It had been the cruelest coincidence, one that surely never should have happened, that another cab had pulled up, waiting for another resident departing the small condo block.

He guessed on a Saturday night, that had not been unexpected. People were going out. Partying, in places where scents mingled - so many scents. Food, wine, cologne, perfume.

There had been some confusion, the hunter remembered. She'd approached the cab expectantly, and in fact she'd almost climbed inside it.

She'd spoken to the driver. There had been laughter - more from her side, although even the cab driver had given a reluctant smile. And then, a tall young man had come walking out. He'd been the one who had booked this first cab.

While the hunter waited, trying to remain calm and contain his anger at such a terrible coincidence, the two had spoken - for a couple of long minutes that had felt like hours to him.

And then, as the man had gotten into his cab and pulled away, the next cab had arrived to ferry his prey safely to her destination.

An unfortunate set of circumstances. Unfair and unjust. It should not have happened, but it had. He'd felt unreasonably anxious about it. On top of everything else, it had seemed like a bad omen and he'd felt the need to make it right as soon as he could.

He wasn't going to give up. Perhaps fortune would favor him this morning, especially since he had everything ready that he needed.

The stick he used to stun his victims was in place. He stunned them only lightly with it, an art he'd perfected over the years. It was by no means a killing blow. He wanted them living and breathing when he applied the bottle of Joy to their chests, to their clothing, soaking them in it.

He needed the warmth of their bodies to interact with that perfume, sending out the scent of rose petals and jasmine that he remembered so well.

She'd beaten him, sometimes viciously, always unstoppably. And the more angry she got, the more emotional she became, the more that perfume had emanated from her in waves, creating a wall of fragrance that felt as evil as an attack. Never could he forget it.

The pain. The abuse. The neglect he'd suffered, all underscored by the luscious, intense waves of that cruelly memorable scent.

He knew that his interval was increasing now, that he was capturing his prey more often, and there was a reason for this. A good reason.

In the past, this perfume had been freely available, though difficult to obtain, with only a certain limited edition release being available each year. But even so, the hunter had sourced one bottle, maybe two. It was enough for him.

It was enough to set his ghosts and demons to rest as he looked into his prey's unconscious face, pouring that almost priceless perfume over the women, drenching their clothing and chest, breathing in the scent he remembered and hated so much.

He would relive those memories again. The violence. The abuse. He would let them fill his mind. Those terrible words, the cuts, the lacerations, the hissed threats. All scorched in his psyche, hurting him, haunting him.

And then, using a soft blanket dotted with the remainder of the perfume, he would smother his victims, killing the memories once and for all.

And then he would bury them in a field of flowers, befitting their youth and beauty, hoping that the flowers would somehow prevent the demons from returning again, even though they crept back inexorably over the months, forcing him to kill again.

But now there had been an unthinkable tragedy.

The perfume he needed, he craved, was no longer being manufactured. He could not believe it. How could such a thing happen? How could a famous scent, sold for many decades, be discontinued?

He'd read and researched. The company had been sold. It was a financial decision. Joy would be no more. A new perfume with the same name was available but it was a completely different scent. It was not the intense, unforgettable fragrance he craved and hated, but yet needed.

In desperation he'd tried to source and buy as many bottles as he could, knowing that his time to obtain them was limited, that there were now finite bottles left in the world.

He had a stockpile now, but even so, he was panicking inside. And the panic was making him want to act more often, to try and get the better of his demons once and for all, because eventually the day would come when this perfume was gone, and no more could be obtained.

And so, in his desperation, his need, he was driving past her condo again, hoping she might be there, and that the elements would align for him at last.

And there she was. His heart skipped a beat as he spotted her. She was walking from the small grocery store opposite, back to the apartment block.

Her hair swung and shone in the morning sun. She wore jeans and a pretty, red top. She looked lightly made up. He glanced around, knowing how risky this was, that it was unplanned but necessary.

He had his stick in the passenger seat, and a bottle of the precious, priceless perfume in his jacket pocket.

He turned off the car engine, took a deep breath, glanced in the rearview mirror, and stepped out of the car, grasping the stick. She turned to face him. He saw the moment of surprise in her eyes. Not fear, he was not a scary looking person. Just surprise.

And then, doubt and fear, as she saw the stick, and that he was approaching her with intent.

"Come here," he muttered.

"No!" she cried, sounding terrified, but she didn't have a chance to say more.

He was upon her before she had a chance to react. He crushed his hand over her mouth to stifle the cries, and then, an instant later, she was in his arms, and being dragged toward the trunk of his car, shielding her with his body in case anyone should see them in that instant when he was doing his work.

As soon as he had her by the car, he struck the back of her head with the stick, silencing her yells of fear and anger. Once she was immobilized, he reached into her jeans pocket and took her phone.

Then he placed her in the trunk. He could see the long, tapered curve of her ear, the smooth skin of her neck, and even the contour of her lips. His prey. Captured at last.

Breathing hard, feeling filled with triumph, he closed the trunk, throwing the stick into the passenger seat. He hadn't hit her hard. Its end was not even bloody this time.

She'd been lightly stunned, and he knew a stunned victim might stay unconscious only a few minutes, and then would wake up. He needed to get far away before that happened, out of range, so there was no chance she could make a noise and sound the alert.

He hoped he'd done a good enough job, in his haste.

But this was the start of a new era. He was going to go to a fresh burial ground, a beautiful field, deep in the forest. She would be the first one to grace it. He hoped that it would be hidden and undiscovered for years to come.

In those flowers, he would smother her.

With his foot hard on the gas pedal, the hunter swerved back onto the road and sped toward his destination.

CHAPTER TWENTY SEVEN

The perfumery manager turned back to May, his face intent and alive with excitement.

"Here's the perfume original. May I apply a little on you? Then you can also tell me what you think about the similarity."

"Sure," May said, glad of the chance to be able to tell for herself that there was a match between the two.

"I'll apply it to your skin, because as I said, this perfume is concentrated and we don't want to stain your clothing."

He touched the stopper to the inside of May's wrist.

Immediately, she smelled it. She drew her breath in, and saw Owen's excitement reflected in her eyes.

Without a doubt this was the same scent. It was so rich, so strong, so distinctive. Not a light or forgettable fragrance. It was powerful and intense and she was convinced that it was the same one she had breathed in earlier.

"It's the same one," Owen said.

Like her, he sounded absolutely certain.

There was absolutely no doubt in either of their minds. This was the scent the killer was using.

"Do you have a record of your sales of it?" May asked.

But the manager shook his head sadly.

"Unfortunately, the previous store manager didn't keep records. I was only promoted to this position a year and a half ago, and by then, all our stock was sold and we couldn't obtain more. It had already been grabbed up by other stores and online sites. I would have gotten some if I could, but sadly, it wasn't my decision," he said regretfully.

"We'll have to investigate the other stores then. But you've been enormously helpful," May said.

"I'm very glad of that. It makes me feel better about this tragedy to think that we at the perfumery counter might be responsible for saving future lives." Josh looked pleased and proud to have been able to give them this important lead.

With this department store a dead end, May knew that they would need to do things the hard way. They'd have to head back to the Fairshore police department, and between herself and Owen, they would need to figure out who had been buying up this perfume, and whether they could trace the killer through his purchases.

As they rushed back to the car, May felt more and more convinced that this represented a turning point in the case. It was finally a way they could use to track him.

*

Just ten minutes later, after a rushed drive back to Fairshore, May and Owen burst into the police department. May was still breathless after running up the road. There was still no parking available close to the police department, and the lobby was filled with police from all local precincts, as well as FBI.

Where was Kerry, May wondered. Was she still busy with the interrogation of their latest suspect?

"Agent Kerry Moore went out just now," the officer at the lobby desk filled May in, correctly interpreting that she'd want to know where her sister was. "She left the suspect in the holding cells for now, and is with the forensic team near the latest burial site. They thought they might have a lead to the killer's vehicle from a nearby gas station camera, so they're seeing if they can get footage."

"I hope so," May said, feeling glad that Kerry was pursuing such a different angle. Surely, out of these two lines of investigation, one would bear fruit?

But for now, they needed to pursue the other. They threaded their way through the packed corridors and went into the back office.

May's desk had been pushed up next to another and was being used for an impromptu meeting space. Only Owen's desk was free. May sat down and they opened their laptops.

"Our best bet is to contact the major distributors of this perfume in Minnesota. That's where he would have looked first, I'm sure," Owen said.

"He might have traveled statewide to source bottles, or even ordered online," May added. "If he ordered online, he could have ordered from anywhere in the country. But maybe he would have chosen local suppliers first."

After the elation that had filled her when they'd learned about this perfume, May was now worried that this was going to end up being like a hunt for a needle in a haystack.

It was a Sunday and she knew this would not make their job any easier. But if this killer had been buying up the perfume bottles, he surely would have bought as many as he could, from whoever had the scent in stock. All they needed to do was get hold of one outlet where he was a repeat customer. And what they did know, beyond any doubt, was that he lived in this area. He was familiar with the local area. For all May knew, he might even live in Fairshore itself, or in neighboring Chestnut Hill.

"Online sales might be easier to start with," May said. "They might have a better record of customers. The perfume itself will allow us to narrow down the suppliers, as it's so scarce. We just need to see if it has been in stock or not. If we don't find local suppliers, we can start looking nationally."

"The other department stores might also have kept a record of people requesting an expensive perfume," Owen said thoughtfully. "They might well have an online facility also. Perhaps we could call the ones in Minneapolis"

"Okay. I'll start with the online sales, and you start with the department stores."

She felt relieved that they had a plan in place, even though it was a sketchy one that was going to be complicated by the fact it was now early afternoon on a Sunday.

But even so, only research would get them where they needed to be. It might be difficult but May promised herself it would not be impossible.

She wouldn't let it be so.

May embarked on her search for the perfume they needed.

She immediately saw that there were two online distributors in the local area of Tamarack County.

One was Perfumes Galore, and the other was Scentsations. Both of them offered online perfume sales with same-day delivery. She was sure that would have suited an impatient psychopath.

May checked the websites, feeling curious, wondering if they had stock of the Joy perfume that she needed.

She was interested to see that both the online sales outlets were out of stock of that perfume, but both seemed to have had it in stock in the past. And that made her hopeful that the killer had visited these sites and had bought at least some of the now finished stock.

So, how to get hold of these sites?

May looked at the bottom of the first one, Perfumes Galore, searching for the contact details.

There was a phone number, but when she dialed it, it rang through to a voicemail, with a message that this number would only be available during office hours.

There was an office address, but it was in an industrial area and May was sure that if they visited the premises they would find them locked up for the weekend.

May left a voice message, with her personal phone number, hoping that by some miracle, the messages would be attended to before tomorrow morning. But she didn't hold out a lot of hope.

Then she disconnected, and turned to the other one, Scentsations.

May felt frustrated to see that this site had a similar setup. It almost looked to have been designed by the same person. There were also no personal contact details.

She dialed the office number and left a similar message.

Then she put her chin in her hands, sighing in frustration as she listened to Owen finishing off his call.

"No luck," he told her regretfully. "I've now spoken to both the major department stores. One doesn't keep the details of all the customers, and another one has a list of loyalty fans, but they can't access it. It's only accessible through head office and head office is closed today." He sighed.

"This is such bad timing," May lamented. "But there must be another way around this. There has to be. This isn't just a website. There are people who run it. People who own it."

And that gave her an idea.

May returned to her keyboard, and this time she did a different search.

She searched for, "Scentsations - Owner."

May narrowed her eyes as the results flashed up. Aha. Here were some results she could work with. There were some media articles that reported on 'prominent local businesswoman Pam Tillery,' who had started out with online fragrances, and recently expanded into skincare and beauty products as well.

"I believe the success of cosmetics is going to be driven by online sales," Pam said to the website interviewing her. "I have a passion for making skincare and fragrances accessible to all!"

Now, it was time to see if May could find out who Pam Tillery was and where in Tamarack County she lived.

"Owen, I've got a name," she said, as her deputy put the phone down again, looking discouraged. "Pam Tillery. We need to get address details for her, or a personal phone number. If we can do that, we might be able to contact her after hours."

"Now that's a great idea." Owen looked hopeful at the prospect of being able to track down one of the site owners.

"I'll go into the police database and see if I can find anything on her," Owen said. "If you search general online results, that covers all bases."

"Pam Tillery, Pam Tillery."

May went into the search engine again and looked for any evidence that might point the way to who she was. Why could they find nothing on her?

And then, a result came up that showed her an alternative way forward.

"I've found something here," she said. "She's married to prominent local footwear distributor Wayne Hart. She must have kept her maiden name. So let's look for Wayne Hart."

"I've got him!" Owen said after a few moments of frenzied searching. "I've got what looks like a current address for Wayne Hart. There's no phone number on record, but May, he lives near here, in Sunnybrook. That's not far; it's a twenty minute drive. Shall we go there and see if Wayne, or better still, Pam, is at home?"

"I think we need to do that," May said.

Their intricate maneuvering through the online world had come up with only one result, and May found herself pinning her hopes on it.

If Pam Tillery was at home, and she had records of her online sales, there was surely a chance that the killer's name would be among them.

CHAPTER TWENTY EIGHT

This was their last hope, their last avenue of research that might be possible today, May knew, as she and Owen sped to Pam Tillery's home in Sunnybrook. And with the potential shortage of perfume and the killer's panicked reaction in speeding up his interval, every hour that this case was unsolved represented a risk he would kill again.

But she didn't want to think that.

It was too dire a thought to contemplate. May felt as if she was protecting the future of every young woman with a flower name, as she gripped the wheel, racing down the road, which was quiet and serene on a Sunday afternoon.

"This had better work out," she muttered to Owen.

"I'm not giving up hope," Owen said. "We have to keep going and we have to keep believing we can catch this guy. All we need is one more piece of the puzzle, and this case could all come together. We just need to find this link to him."

They headed into Sunnybrook, and May found herself crossing fingers that Pam Tillery would be home.

Wayne Hart's house was at the end of Ridge Road. These homes were large and luxurious, May saw, with huge yards. Being situated on a ridge, the homes had a panoramic view over the shimmering waters of Eagle Lake, which looked like a calm and peaceful place when bathed in mild afternoon sun.

They stopped outside the ornate main gate of number 1, Ridge Road, and May rang the bell.

They waited. May found she was actually holding her breath in anticipation. Would anyone be home? Would the bell be answered?

Looking inside, the place looked quiet, and she felt fear clench her stomach again.

And then, finally, a man's voice came over the intercom. He sounded grumpy, as if he'd been woken from an afternoon nap by the piercing noise of the buzzer.

"Who is it?" he snapped.

"It's Deputies Moore and Lovell from the police department," May explained politely. "We're looking for Pam Tillery. We need her help with a case."

"What?" the man said, sounding incredulous. May was sure he'd heard her just fine. It was more an expression of surprise.

The intercom went dead. She and Owen glanced at each other. The minute's pause seemed to last an eternity. Then May caught her breath as the front door opened. A gray-haired man looked out at them. Although he was some distance away down the long drive, May had the sense he was frowning. Then he pressed a buzzer and the gate slid back.

Quickly, May drove through the gate and onto the long, tree lined drive. Gravel scrunched under the car's tires as she approached the house. She parked under the shade of an elm tree and climbed out. May approached the house feeling intensely nervous.

"Are you Wayne Hart?" she asked the gray-haired man politely.

"I am, but what on earth is this about? I did not expect this," he grumbled. "We've just gotten back from an overseas trip this morning. Are you sure you have the right house?"

He was wearing tracksuit pants and a T-shirt and, from the rumpled state of his hair, had definitely just climbed out of bed.

"We definitely do have the right house," May said, feeling intensely relieved at this timing. "I'd be so thankful if Pam was able to help us now."

"Well, I guess you can come in."

Wayne stepped aside, and May and Owen walked into the large, tiled hall. He gestured to a door on his right and they walked into a lounge with a panoramic view of the lake, gray furniture, and a large chandelier.

May sat down on a gray sofa with Owen next to her. Wayne stomped to the foot of the stairs.

"Pam," he called. "Some police officers are here. I don't know what they want, but they say they're here to see you."

The man turned and looked at them again, and May was sure he was sizing them up. Even so, May felt deeply relieved that they'd managed to get this far.

"I'll come down," Pam Tillery called back. And then she appeared, walking down the stairs.

She looked to be in her fifties, tall and slender, with platinum-blonde hair and an elegant demeanor. She was wearing a Japanese robe, and pretty, jeweled sandals.

"What is this about?" she asked curiously as she entered the lounge.

"We're investigating the recent killings," May said, trying to keep her voice calm and level.

"Are those all the bodies that have been found in graves?" Pam asked, sounding puzzled. "I heard about that before we left France."

"Yes. That's the case we're working on, and I think you might be able to help us."

"Me?" Pam looked astounded. Wayne's frown deepened.

"We know that you sell perfume online and we think you might have some online records that would be useful to us," Owen explained.

Pam stared at Wayne for a moment looking totally confused.

"I really don't see how I can help you. My online records? How can they solve this crime? They're at the office, anyway."

May's heart plummeted. Surely they couldn't be stalled now, by this couple, who were so surprised by the police arriving that they were not in a frame of mind to be cooperative. She knew she'd have to do her best to persuade them they needed to help.

"We think the killer may have been buying up a very rare, expensive perfume. Called Joy, by Jean Patou. It's been discontinued."

"Yes, it has. But you're wearing it now, aren't you? I can actually smell it on your skin," Pam said. "I've got a very good nose for my perfumes."

"The department store applied it earlier today while we were checking if it was the scent that was involved in the crimes," May admitted.

"And it is? How?" Pam asked.

"He uses it when he kills his victims," May explained. "It must either be a trigger for killing, or else a signature of some kind. Both are common in serial killer murders, which these definitely are."

Pam's eyebrows shot up. "Seriously? This is - well, this is spooky. And you think he bought from my site?"

"We don't know, but we are theorizing he may have been looking to stockpile the perfume, since it's becoming harder to get a hold of. And he may have ordered from you."

"Well, can I have a look tomorrow and let you know?" Pam said.

She was clearly reluctant to interrupt her relaxing afternoon at home, and May thought she simply didn't realize the urgency of this case.

"Ma'am, every minute counts," she pleaded. "The FBI has a team on site. The police are working around the clock. And all of us are terrified that this killer might capture another victim at any time. He's escalating the speed of his kills."

"The sooner we can catch him, the sooner everyone in this county can be safe," Owen added emphatically.

Pam sighed. "I don't have all the records with me. But I can look up the recent sales on my laptop. For the past three or four months, I think. I should have those available and I can give them to you now. We did have Joy in stock, until about a month ago."

"That will be great. If we look through, we can see if any of them are likely to be the killer," May said.

"Well, let me get my laptop," Pam said.

She turned and headed back upstairs.

Wayne remained, still frowning at them as if he hadn't quite forgiven them for interrupting his nap, despite the urgent circumstances.

As she waited, May went over the parameters in her mind, thinking of what they were looking for.

The killer lived locally. He was a man. And it was very likely that he'd bought more than one of these perfumes because he would be looking to hoard them.

May was sure plenty of men bought perfumes online as gifts, and many of these might live locally. For her, the key issue was going to be multiple purchases. That was what would differentiate this man from the other customers.

As she waited, May's phone rang.

"Excuse me," she said, getting up and hurrying outside to take the call. It was the officer at the front desk of the Fairshore police department, she saw.

"Hi, Tim," she said quickly, as soon as she was outside in the sunny front yard.

"Hi, May." Officer Tim's voice was tense and urgent. "I thought I'd better call you straight away. We have just had a call come in from a local man, Vic Easton, who lives in Chestnut Hill."

"What did he say?" May said. From the tone of Tim's voice, this was not good news.

"He said something weird had happened. He said last night he met a girl from his condo block when they were both waiting for cabs to go out," Tim explained.

"Go on?" May asked.

"They got to chatting, and organized a meet-up at her place today, at three. He got a message from her at five to three, asking what he wanted to drink, and that she was quickly going across the road to the grocery store, and would be back at three. So he told her."

"And then?" May asked, but she was already dreading how this story might play out.

"He arrived just now and she wasn't there. Her apartment is locked up. He can't geta hold of her on her phone; it's turned off. She's not across the road. He can't see her anywhere."

"Is he worried that she's gone missing?" May asked, feeling icy cold inside.

"Yes. He is very worried. And now, so am I, because he gave us her name. Her name is Primrose Eliot, and I'm very worried, May. It's a flower name. What if she'd the killer's next target?"

May took a deep breath. Her worst fears were playing out. Undoubtedly, the killer had captured another victim. His ferocious need to kill was unstoppable.

And they were too late, too far behind to be able to prevent another death, unless somehow, by a miracle, they could catch up.

CHAPTER TWENTY NINE

May rushed back into the elegant home, where Pam Tillery represented her last hope for catching the killer. Primrose Eliot had been targeted and taken, but this had been done so recently that they surely must have a chance to catch up with him.

This killer killed within hours, but not within minutes. He couldn't do that, because he had to take the victims where he needed them to be. He needed to pour that perfume on their warm, living skin, dousing them in it and breathing it in before he smothered them. That would have to be done at the site where he buried them, and couldn't be done in the trunk of a car.

So by now, May guessed, Primrose would be knocked out and in the back of his car, speeding away to a burial site.

But the FBI and local police were swarming around three of his chosen sites. Did he have more locations in mind - either used, or earmarked? If so, where would they be? Had he prepared a grave already or was he doing things differently now, in his haste and panic?

May had no answers to these questions. But as she saw Pam Tillery walk downstairs carrying a white laptop, she hoped she might get the answer to the most important question of all - the killer's identity.

Owen glanced at her anxiously. He clearly felt the waves of stress that were emanating from her.

"There's been another woman taken," May blurted out. She couldn't stop herself. Owen sat straight, his face a picture of consternation.

"Another?" he said, his voice incredulous.

Hearing his tone, even Wayne's frown disappeared. And Pam's eyes widened as she rushed the last few steps into the lounge, quickly opening her laptop.

"Another victim taken?" Wayne asked. "You mean, this killer's just captured someone else? Just now?"

Finally, May saw, the seriousness of the situation had hit home.

"She's just been grabbed. Probably fifteen minutes ago," May said. She knew she sounded breathless. She felt like bursting into tears of utter panic. But she knew that the only possible way of finding this killer, of catching up with this evil man, would be to remain calm and strong.

Pam was now deep in her own laptop, the data set up ready for her to look through.

"Okay. Sales of Joy. What are we looking for?" she asked. She also sounded, now, as if she was highly stressed and also battling for calmness.

"We're looking for local buyers in this area. We're looking for men. And especially, we're looking for anyone who might have bought more than one bottle," May said.

"Right. Let's start with the sales themselves, as we don't sell much of that particular perfume."

Pam stared down at her screen, tapping keys lightly.

"We've had just five sales of that perfume in the past few months. Now that I think of it, that is higher than usual, with all our stock bought out. Of those, four have been local, within Minnesota. And it looks like three have been to men."

She stared more closely at the screen. "But none have bought multiple bottles. Only one purchase each. Perhaps he didn't choose this site?" She looked at May with a mixture of doubt and hope.

"Can I please have a look?" May asked.

"Sure. Here are the records." Pam turned her laptop to face May.

Immediately, Owen scooted over, and May knew that her deputy's analytical mind would be invaluable in helping work out who the killer was.

"Three men. Their names are Stanley Seeger, Dan O'Donnell, and Victor Easton. And let's take a look at where they live." Owen sounded cool and factual.

May felt grateful for her deputy's calmness. She felt frantic inside. All she could think of was that the killer would be getting closer and closer to his destination. The window of time they had to save Primrose was narrowing drastically.

"Now this is interesting," Owen said. "I'm picking up something here."

"What?" May asked.

"They all seem to have the same delivery address, according to these records. I'm wondering if the killer might have used different names when he ordered, to avoid anyone picking up at a glance that he was buying multiple bottles."

"He could have done that, I guess," Pam agreed, nodding. "There's nothing on our site to stop a buyer from doing that, but the credit card details would obviously be in the payer's name."

"What's the address?" May asked. "Is it close to here?"

"Yes. It's on the outskirts of Lakeview. It's very close by, May." Owen sounded excited. "And since these were paid for by credit card, we can take a look at the card details - if you don't mind, ma'am?" He turned to Pam.

"No, I don't mind at all. Please do." Now both Pam and Wayne were looking as fixated on this chase as May felt.

"Okay. The card's in another name, and again, it's the same person who paid for all three bottles. Brian Blanchard. So he's our man. Our new person of interest. Brian Blanchard, of twelve Lake Terrace, in Lakeview. That's where we need to go, May, as fast as possible."

May jumped to her feet.

"Thank you so much. You've been incredibly helpful in finding this lead. Thank you," she said again, before turning and running out of the house, with Owen hot on her heels.

"Good luck!" Wayne called, now clearly caught up in the thrill of the chase. "Hope you find him!"

They pounded to the car, and May accelerated down the driveway. They needed to find Brian, but the chances of him being home were slim. So after confirming that, as fast as possible, they needed to figure out where he was.

May got on the phone to Kerry as she drove. Now, she needed her sister's help, and for the full might of the FBI to help take this forward.

"May, you got any news? We're not picking up much here. The gas station owner is out hiking and he's the only one with the keys to the office where the camera footage is kept." Kerry sounded in a foul mood. May hoped the news she was about to tell her sister would improve it.

"Yes, I do. We've found him. At least, I think so. His name is Brian Blanchard. He lives in Lakeview. We're on our way to his address now, but he just grabbed another victim from a residence in Chestnut Hill. So we need to know what vehicle Brian Blanchard owns, and we need to get an APB out on it. We're right next door to Lakeview so we'll check his residence now, but I don't think he would have gone home. I think he's driving straight to one of the burial sites. And perhaps he's picked a new one."

"I'm on it," Kerry said immediately. "We'll look this guy up straight away, find out what he drives, and get the APB out. I'll let you know as soon as I know. And we'll send another team to search his house."

She cut the call, and May returned her full focus to her furious race along the road.

She was glad that she had Kerry in her corner. Her sister was like a lightning bolt when it came to organizing things. She'd get everyone moving at top speed, May knew.

Just a minute later, Lakeview came into sight. He lived on the outskirts, according to where their coordinates were taking them. They had found his house, at least.

"There it is!" May said, as a pretty suburban home came into view. "Let's stop by the entrance, and we can see whether he's home. I think we need to assume he isn't."

May pulled in and put the car in park. She got out and stood in front of the house.

She could see immediately that Brian wasn't at home. The white-painted garage door was open, and there was no car in sight. He must have left, fast. In a hurry. Too much of a hurry to even close his garage.

May knew deep in her bones that he'd been preoccupied with the new hunt for yet another victim. He'd been rushing to capture Primrose. They had needed to look, but she'd been ready for this disappointment. What was more important, now, was to take the next step.

"I'm guessing he's already driving to the site. Wherever it is. So where do we go now? Which one do we try for?"

The picture of May's map came into her mind, with the shaded areas that she and Owen had thought of where the burial sites might be. She remembered the few sites they had thought were likely, but had not yet explored. The problem was they were all in different places. One was far north of Chestnut Hill. There were two others to the south which were close by. May had picked one, Owen the other. And there was another one to the far west.

He might be choosing any of the obvious sites, or else he might have found one that was entirely his own, and which neither May nor Owen had thought of.

Where to start? They had to start somewhere. May looked at Owen. Which direction gave the best chance of success?

"South," they said, exactly at the same time. May felt glad they'd both thought the same way.

They climbed back in the car and May sped off down the road. They were already heading south, so all they needed to do was to follow this route. She had no idea whether their plan would succeed, but if there was a chance, they had to try.

And then, May's phone rang.

It was Kerry.

"Right, sis," she said briskly, but May could hear the tension simmering in her voice. "We have looked up his car. It's a red Ford SUV. I'm sending you the plate now. Which direction are you checking?"

"We're heading south," May said.

"We'll send out teams to the north and the west in that case. Stay in touch and be careful. We'll communicate on the radio from now on, so all teams can stay in touch."

Already, the radio was crackling with updates as police in the area tuned in, giving their location and direction.

May began to feel a glimmer of hope that somehow they might find this man before he killed again, that they might manage to rescue this one final victim whose life was in such peril now.

The first site was just ten minutes away. The area they were driving through was increasingly hilly, with sharp bends in the road, steep drops, and meadows and gorges filled with flowers among the forested slopes.

But then, with a cry, Owen grabbed her arm, pointing to a deep valley.

"May! I think I see something down there."

"What is it?"

"I don't know. I got a glimpse of it. But it was something red, and now I'm wondering if it might have been a red car roof. Should we take the next turning to the right and check it out? There's a lot of flowers down there."

May agonized over the choice. Time was tight. But it was worth checking this out. For sure. If they were wrong, they'd lose time. But if this was Brian Blanchard's SUV, they might save a life.

May swung the car to the right and powered down the twisting road.

CHAPTER THIRTY

The car accelerated through the hairpin bends, with May's hands tight on the wheel and her foot pressed on the gas. She was having to focus all her attention on driving this narrow, precarious route, but managed to glance to the right, and saw what Owen had seen as they rounded a dizzying bend. She caught her breath.

A red-roofed car was parked in the valley. From this vantage point, it was impossible to see what type it was. She was amazed that the sharp-eyed Owen had even seen it.

As they got closer, they'd be able to check the model of the car. And if it was wrong, they could peel away and continue the hunt.

But it was the right color of car. That alone made it worth checking because red cars were not so common.

A cold chill went through her as her imagination leaped ahead, considering the scenarios. Was Brian already at the site where he was planning to kill? Had he already struck? Was he in the process of burying his latest victim?

Were they too late?

"You see, May," Owen's breathless voice interrupted her thoughts. "I don't think he's going to choose a site so close to the road again. I think we might be in time, this time. He must be really pissed that we're discovering all his secrets."

"You think? So he might pick somewhere further away?" May asked.

"Yeah, I think he might do that. He might be looking to outwit us, and create a new, hidden site. That's how he'll be. He's sneaky. He's always been a step ahead. I guess he's looking to get back to that position now."

They rounded the final curve, swooping down the incline to the gravel road that led off the narrow blacktopped lane.

"It's the right car. A Ford Explorer," May gasped. It was parked right at the edge of the woods.

"What's the plate? Does it check out?" she asked. She felt breathless with tension. Owen's observant eyes had caught the car in literally the only moment it had been visible from the main road above.

"It's the same plate," Owen replied, checking his phone. May could hear excitement and stress thrumming in his voice.

Quickly, Owen got on the radio, notifying the others.

"We found him. He's parked here, just outside the woods." He read out the coordinates. "There's no sign of him, no sign of the victim. We're taking this forward as fast as we can. Please, bring all the teams here, as quickly as you can get to this site."

May jumped out of the car, breathing in the summer-warm air. It was a hot day, and humid, but it was also peaceful. The woods looked deep and cool.

Looking at the position of the car, and the lack of any pathway or footprints visible in the long grass, there was no other place he could have gone but into the forest, where a narrow trail showed the route. That was where he was taking her, May felt sure. He'd changed up his modus operandi and gone for a more hidden burial ground, deep in the woods. May was sure that the clearings in these damp, low-lying trees would be filled with profusions of wildflowers, and he would find many sites that would fit his needs in here.

But he would have to walk in, and go a long way, carrying a body. That would slow him down. Perhaps it would allow them to catch him.

Owen was already striding towards the trail, just a few yards away, which led into the woods. May followed him, her heart pounding.

The path was narrow and rough. At a glance, May realized reluctantly that it would not hold footprints. The canopy of trees covered it, and it wound its way between them so that they could not see far ahead.

The forest was peaceful. It smelled sweet. May could smell the perfume of wildflowers, and earth, and green leaves. The silence here was deep and complete. Even the birdsong sounded muted here.

They moved quickly, but cautiously, keeping their eyes on the ground, and then looking from side to side into the deeper forest, trying not to miss any clue.

May couldn't shake the vision of Brian, this man she didn't know as a person but only as a force of evil, sneaking into the forest with Primrose's unconscious form over his shoulder, a shovel in his hand, and murderous intent in his heart.

It was a mistake to think he would make it easy for them to find him. Brian was cunning and ruthless. He would go to extreme lengths to make sure they did not get him. That's who he was.

Where was he going to get rid of the body?

Had he prepared a grave, or was he going in here blind, forging a path, deciding as he went where he was going to place her?

May knew they could not risk missing any place where he might have turned off the path, but so far she'd seen no chance for that in the overgrowth of brush and ferns. They rushed along the path, going as fast as they dared. May's senses were wide open. She was trying to hear the slightest rustling, the tiniest noise in the undergrowth. The thump-thump of a shovel and scrape of earth was the sound she dreaded to hear, but she hadn't picked it up yet.

And then, they reached a point in the trail where it split left and right.

May was breathing hard. Although they'd been walking fast, the cool air in these woods was prickling her spine. She stared from left to right, and down at the ground. There was no indication which way he'd gone. The ground was softer here, covered in leaves, but there were no discernible prints to see. Perhaps a tracker could pick up subtle signs, but not her.

"We need to choose. Left or right?" she whispered. "Do we each take one?"

"Yes, I guess we'll have to," Owen said. "I don't like the idea of us splitting up, but we can't waste any time. We can't risk the both of us going down the wrong track. Not when there's so little time."

"Okay then," May breathed. "I'll take the left side."

"I'll take right. We need to keep in contact, May. If you see or hear anything, message me. And I'll do the same. Keep your gun out."

"You do the same. Please, stay safe," May said.

She also didn't like the idea of going separate ways, but the urgency of this crisis made it imperative.

She looked into Owen's eyes. He returned her gaze.

"I care for you, May. I really do, and I want you to know that," he said softly.

And May's heart accelerated because she saw an honesty in his expression she'd never seen before.

"I care for you, too," she said in a small voice, her heart now hammering with the immensity of what this meant.

But there was no time left for more of these words that meant so much, and action was now imperative.

Turning away from him, she headed down the left-hand track, moving as fast as she could. They'd seen no sign of the killer as yet, but that fit in with what she guessed he might do, moving deep into the woods to hide his victim, choosing a new site that would not be found.

She imagined him, his legs surely burning, grasping the unconscious girl as he strode, focused on his burial site and rituals. He would have the perfume with him. In his pocket, perhaps. That was a certainty. May's spine contracted at the terrible thought, and she pushed the vision aside.

Had she heard a footfall ahead? She stopped dead, listening. She thought she had, but now that she was standing still, the woods were blanketed in silence again.

She paced forward, moving more carefully now.

As the minutes passed, and May wound her way ever deeper into the woods, she started to think she was on the wrong track, and that Owen had chosen the right route. Because there was nothing to be found here. She must have gone a mile alone. Perhaps it was time to turn back. If Owen had chosen the right way, he could be coming face to face with the killer at any moment.

May slowed, breathing hard, feeling overwhelmed with the implications this decision would have.

And then, the glitter of silver gleamed in a patch of sunshine ahead.

Staring at it, May paced forward. It was a delicate silver chain. It was lying in the trail, with the sun sparkling on it, almost like a beacon pointing the way.

May couldn't shake the image of that chain being pulled from Primrose's throat, perhaps after being caught on something, as the killer adjusted his grip.

And then, she stopped again, her senses sparking with adrenaline. She'd heard something ahead.

Something that got her spine prickling. Something she'd never, ever expected to hear.

It was a muffled choking noise, almost inaudible. But most definitely it was a woman's voice. It was coming from further down the track, where May could see a small, leafy clearing in the trees.

Her heart was banging in her throat as she crept forward. Had Primrose regained consciousness; was she trying to cry for help? Had the killer left her here and gone somewhere nearby, to prepare a grave?

May knew this might be her only chance to save the victim.

She'd dreaded that she had been killed already, that they would find the body buried. She'd prepared herself for that. She'd been steeling herself for that truth.

But suddenly, there was hope. Despite the danger, if she was quick and quiet, she had a chance to save this captured woman.

CHAPTER THIRTY ONE

There she was! May couldn't believe it. As she paced silently into the clearing, she saw that Primrose was there in front of her. She was blindfolded, her hands were fastened tightly behind her and wrapped around the trunk of a tree, and a thick gag in her mouth was preventing her from uttering more than the softest moan. There was a rope around her neck, holding her tightly to the tree.

Worse still, in her efforts to free herself, the rope around her neck had tightened, almost lethally. In horror, May saw that she was on the point of suffocation. Between the rope and the gag, Primrose could barely breathe. She was close to losing consciousness, May saw. She was choking violently, her shoulders heaving.

This was now an emergency. She had to get the rope and the gag off this woman's neck. There was no time to do anything but save her.

There was no sight of Brian, no sound of him. She was sure that he was somewhere in the area, digging a grave in the soft soil. She'd gotten here just in time to be able to save a life.

May rushed forward, hoping she could get this woman freed, and breathing easily, as soon as she could.

Primrose was choking and coughing through her gag, in a panic, her shoulders hunched, her breath rasping and rattling in her throat. With shaking hands, May quickly worked to get the gag out of her mouth. The woman flinched when May touched her, and she realized that sudden touch, in her darkness, must have been terrifying.

She peeled the gag away. It was wet with saliva. Primrose gasped in another shallow, rattling breath. Removing the gag hadn't helped much. The main problem was that she was choking from the rope.

Feeling frantic, May undid her blindfold, so at least she could see she was being helped. Blinking in what must have felt like dazzling light after the darkness he'd plunged her into, her wide green eyes met May's in a desperate appeal.

Then, May hastily fumbled her penknife out of her pocket. It was now imperative to cut through the rope fastening Primrose's neck, or she would die. Then she could call Owen, and then work on the woman's wrist ties.

"Primrose, I'm here for you," she whispered, as she gently sawed at the rope. "Be very quiet. I'm going to take you out of here."

The woman's breath was coming in harsh gasps. She was shaking with the effort of breathing. Her skin was cold and her face icy pale. May was touched by how young and vulnerable the victim looked. She seemed about twenty-two, severely distressed, and clearly on the point of asphyxiation.

She reached for the penknife, and flipped out the longest blade. It was time to free this woman, as fast as she could.

The rope was thick, knotted. It was tight, and May had to hack at it with her penknife, a slow laborious task. She didn't want to waste any time, but she also didn't want to cut or damage the woman's throat.

It was difficult to cut through. It had been wound around several times, and the blade kept threatening to snap. May had to push hard to get it through. She tucked her gun back in her holster and placed her phone on the ground beside her so that she could use both hands.

She knew that at any second, she might hear footsteps behind her that signaled the killer was coming back. She turned her head this way and that, listening carefully. But at least he clearly wasn't expecting to find her here, and that gave her an advantage.

But finally, she'd managed to cut through that tight, choking rope. She eased it away from Primrose's neck and the woman took a long, rattling gasp of air, wheezing and coughing.

May felt weak with relief that she'd managed to save her from a terrible, ghastly death. And now, it was time to call Owen. She needed to know that help was on the way, before she did another thing.

But as May reached for her phone, she heard a rustle above her head. From the tree above, someone dropped like a stone.

May shrieked as a foot kicked her in the head, so hard that she sprawled down, thumping on the ground, the rough earth and leaves raking her chin and hands.

For a confused moment, she had no idea what had happened. This was all so impossible. She'd seen nothing. Heard nothing. Had it been a falling branch?

But even as her body slammed to the ground in shock, her mind was racing ahead, and in that moment, May knew the killer had her. This entire setup had been a trap, perhaps all the way down to the silvery lure of that necklace.

He had wanted to trap her, knowing that she would be unable to call for help until she'd saved the woman, on the point of death. In that moment, she realized this was the last, desperate stage of his plan, which he was now successfully winging.

Stunned and shocked, she scrambled to get up, knowing it was time to fight or die. But it was too late. A foot slammed down into her shoulder blade, crushing the breath out of her so that she choked and gasped.

A rough hand tugged her gun from her belt and the next thing May knew, it had been tossed into the bushes. She heard a scrape as her phone was kicked away.

She fought for all she was worth, flailing against the foot that was crushing her down, doing her best to writhe from out of his hold.

But he was far too strong. She'd been winded, and he was subduing her with ruthless efficiency. She was pinned down, and the next moment, she felt his hands on her. She'd lost her penknife. That was gone. Her gun was lost.

He was a monster.

More than that, he was clearly an experienced fighter who was good at his job, which was to seize the element of surprise, and overpower his victims quickly and effectively. As May struggled, she was unable to make any inroads against him.

May kicked out, and clawed at the earth, the leafy ground. But still she was unable to escape his hold.

"Help!" she screamed.

"You're a smart lady," he gasped into her ear. "You're a smart one. You figured it out. But you'd better watch it, because if you scream again, then I'm going to hurt her. Not you. Her."

May froze, shocked by that terrible threat. And then, a rope was looping her wrists together and pulling tight behind her back. She knew she was going to have to fight like the devil if she was going to save herself.

She could feel his breath on her neck as he worked on her. The friction of the rope abraded her wrists as he pulled even harder, seeking to immobilize her.

She tried to kick out again, and when he grabbed her knee, she used the opportunity to writhe even farther to the side and away from him.

She kicked out, flailing, trying to head butt him even as she desperately struggled to get the ropes free.

He was strong, still much stronger than her, but she'd hurt him now, and she was desperate to save herself. Her life depended on it. May gritted her teeth, and kicked out again, desperately. If she could hurt him, she might get away! She might yet live. She had to. She could not let this cruelly intelligent man get the better of her.

And then, when she thought she was going to be able to wrench herself free, he grabbed a fistful of her hair and with a sharp, sudden jerk, wrenched her head back.

The sudden pain took her breath away, and in that moment, he pulled the rope tight. Now her hands were pinned behind her back, and he was dragging her to the tree.

He grabbed her by the throat with one hand, his fingers digging into her neck, a move she'd not anticipated, and it made her gasp for breath.

May was coughing too badly to try, choking from the brutal pressure he'd exerted on her throat. Before she could blink, he had looped the rope around the tree, holding the end of it tightly so she could not escape.

In that moment, May could see the killer before her, the monster she'd been tracking. He looked like a normal, average, thirty-something-year-old man, except his face was a mask of rage and twisted intent.

And then, to her shock, the rage evaporated. In its place, she saw an incredulous smile.

"I have you at last," he whispered.

She stared at him in horror, but as she did so, understanding slowly dawned.

Lauren had never been on this man's hit list. Never been his target. But she had. Thanks to her name, he had known about her and known who she was.

"Oh, May. May Moore," he whispered. "What a surprise. I never, ever thought I'd get you. You were only ever someone I dreamed of taking. Your name. May. The flowering shrub. Such pretty, distinctive shrubs, with a profusion of white flowers. Delicate and beautiful. Oh, you were on my list, my little May."

He leaned forward, breathing in deeply, and May remembered with a shiver that she smelled of his triggering scent, Joy.

"You're wearing the perfume I need already," he hissed. "We have to do it, now. That scent brings the demons, and while they are here, you must die, so they can be gone forever."

He leaned close to her, reaching up to the tree, taking down the soft pillow that he'd wedged high in the branches.

Pushing it against her face, he whispered, "May. May Moore, I'm going to kill you now."

CHAPTER THIRTY TWO

May felt paralyzed with horror for a brief, blood-curdling moment. She'd been so wrong. Wrong about everything. Wrong that the killer had wanted Lauren. She'd never realized that she herself had been one of the people on his list.

Owen was far away, searching the other side of the track. She hadn't had the chance to call him, thanks to the clever setup that had lured her straight into the clearing.

She'd done exactly what he'd wanted her to do. It had all been so easy for him.

May had no one to turn to in her moment of mortal danger. She was alone. The killer – this cold, remorseless monster – was right in front of her, and he was going to kill her. He was going to carry out the sentence of a psychopath, someone who had no interest in human life, nor any human feeling.

She was going to die. And then he would kill Primrose, too.

A voice in her head cried out, No! You can't let him! And as May heard Primrose gasp in renewed terror, she knew that this was not an option. No way could she allow this to happen. This victim deserved to live, and May would have to save her.

She wasn't going to die here. Not without a fight.

The longer she fought, the bigger the chance that Owen might end up realizing something was wrong, and turn back to look for May. Her deputy and she often thought the same way. Perhaps, deep inside him, Owen knew.

The longer May could fight, the more time she'd give him to come and find her.

She struggled against the soft pillow with everything she had. She fought its suffocating embrace, twisting and writhing. She kicked out, tried to hurt him with her boot. She flailed and twisted her bound hands, trying to get loose.

But he just laughed, evading her attempts. She was trapped against the tree.

"Struggle all you like," he whispered. "The longer this takes, the more I will enjoy it."

He removed the pillow, adjusted his grasp on it, and May knew he was ready to crush her face with it again, tighter this time.

And then, at that moment, May heard a noise she hadn't expected.

A loud, whirring, slapping noise. The noise of fast-approaching helicopter blades.

Kerry and the FBI were coming - and they weren't coming by car, as May had expected. They were in a chopper that was flying directly overhead, and that gave May the barest edge of a fighting chance. While she could speak, before that pillow came down a second time, she had to use her voice.

Her wits against his.

The helicopter blotted out the sun for a moment, casting a darker shadow into the dim light of the clearing. The noise was loud and threatening. It was flying so low that it was almost at treetop level.

And May realized that if she played her cards right, she had one chance now. Just one chance at a bluff that could buy her enough time to possibly save her life.

"Look there! They've got a gun!" May yelled, staring up at the shadow above. "They're aiming it at you. Goodbye, sucker! The FBI is going to blow you away!"

And Brian hesitated.

He looked up.

Psychopath or not, May realized that he would not have been human not to do that. Everyone was going to look up when a helicopter flew that low overhead, and someone shouted that warning.

And it gave her the chance she needed, the only chance she was going to get.

For just one moment, he was distracted. He took his eyes off her.

May flung herself sideways. But not away from him, not in the direction she'd been pulling, to try and fight the rope.

She launched herself toward him and she kicked out with everything she had, knowing that this was her only chance to strike a blow that would unbalance him, and allow her to start fighting back. This moment, this instant in time, was the only chance she was going to have.

She kicked out in rage and despair, with everything she had.

The tip of her foot connected hard with his knee, and there was a satisfying thud as the sole of her shoe hit his flesh.

And it was a lucky blow. A good kick. Glancing at the sky, he wasn't expecting it.

It knocked Brian off his feet and he sprawled sideways on the ground with a surprised, angry shout. He let go of the pillow, scrabbling for purchase on the leafy ground.

May fought the rope with everything she had, rolling sideways to try and loosen it, struggling for all she was worth, knowing that there was probably not going to be enough time to get free, but trying and fighting all the same.

She'd done it. She'd gotten one of her hands free. Now, she was ready for him. She would take him on. Never mind that he was taller and stronger. With one hand to do it, she'd fight for her life, and she'd fight for Primrose's life, too.

May braced herself, ready for his attack, ready to grab his throat and try to claw his eyes out, to do whatever she could to get the advantage, not allowing herself to think of failure at all.

With an angry roar, he turned to her.

Come try, May thought.

And then, from behind her, she heard the voice she'd longed to hear, but had never allowed herself to hope for.

"Hands in the air! You are under arrest!"

Brian whirled around to face Owen.

For a moment, the air seemed to crackle with tension as Brian considered his options. For a moment, May realized he was thinking of running.

But then, as if his demons wouldn't allow it, as if the driving force that prodded him to kill was too strong, he lunged toward Primrose one more time with a snarl.

"No!" May yanked her other hand free from the ties and scrambled to her feet, diving after him, grabbing his arm, even as Owen sprinted over to tackle the man.

With a yell of fury, he sprawled on the ground. May gritted her teeth. She had soil in her hair, she was dirty, she was battered and bruised, but she wasn't going to let go of his arm again.

But Owen had him now. Brian kicked and plunged, but the tackle had been effective and now he was face-down in the dirt, with Owen dragging his other hand behind his back.

The click of the handcuffs finally signaled that they had managed to subdue one of the most dangerous, tenacious killers they had ever chased down.

With shaking hands, she helped Owen tie him to the tree so that he could not get away before backup arrived.

"I called you," Owen whispered, looking at her with all his feelings there, visible in his face as they pulled the rope tight around the tree. "I called you and when you didn't answer, I got worried and rushed back."

"I'm so glad you did," May whispered back in a heartfelt tone.

Only when she was sure the knots were secure, did she return her focus to Primrose, picking up her knife from the ground and sawing carefully at those tight ropes.

"It's going to be okay," she said in a soft voice, seeing at last that the fear had ebbed from the captive woman's eyes. "You're going to be fine. We've got him at last, and he's never going to harm another woman again."

EPILOGUE

It was just over twenty-four hours later, and May felt like she was in a completely different world.

Instead of being tied up with rope in the middle of the forest, ready to fight for her life, she was in her cottage, picking out the best top to wear, and getting ready to dry her hair.

She was going on a date.

An actual date. With Owen.

He'd asked her again yesterday, in the car on the way back to the police department, as FBI swarmed the forest scene, and the killer was loaded into a police van, ready for transport to the maximum security cell where he would be held.

And May had realized that life was short, and that perhaps the person she wanted to be, the person she was realizing she could be, would not be scared to say yes, and to break out of her restrictive comfort zone, and to change things in a way that might make her happier.

After all, it was only one date. This was just the start of something better and more exciting, and May knew it would be a slow start.

But she was looking forward to tonight, a lot.

The day had been filled with messages of congratulations. Sheriff Jack had personally commended her and Owen at the press conference earlier. The FBI had thanked them for bravery shown and a job well done. Primrose's parents had called her and cried on the phone for about half an hour.

May's mother and father had called her, too.

"May! I heard you fought this killer hand to hand," her mother had said in admiring tones. "You saved the community. I'm so proud of you, angel!"

"As am I," her father had echoed, and May had felt ten feet tall at their praise.

But catching the killer was all the reward she needed. She felt a deep sense of relief that this psychopath would no longer be terrorizing their community. At last, he would be locked away for the rest of his life.

She'd thanked Kerry, whose flyover had unwittingly saved May's life, allowing her to lash back at the killer and giving Owen time to reach her before Brian had suffocated May.

Kerry had given her a big, hard hug before she'd gotten into the car and headed off for their parents, where she would be spending a night with them, breaking the news about her engagement, and May was sure, getting all the love and support she needed at this time.

But May had declined the invitation to join that family gathering, because she was going on a date with Owen.

They were going for dinner, and then they were going dancing. And May was looking forward to it more than she'd believed possible. It felt exciting, as if a new and different life was glimpsed behind a door that was open now, just a crack.

But, as she picked up the hairdryer, May heard her phone ring. Quickly, she rushed over and grabbed it.

It was an unfamiliar number calling, and she answered feeling a flicker of trepidation.

"Deputy May Moore?" the voice said. "It's Pete here, from Pete's Locks. You brought a key in over the weekend. Two keys, actually."

"Yes." May stood straighter, feeling a spark of hope. "Yes, I did. Is there any news on them?"

"I think so. I've been trying to think back over the jobs I've done, and networking with my contacts."

"And is there a result?" May felt breathless with hope.

"Actually, as I was driving home this evening, one of my contacts called me back, and we were able to piece together where this safe is. There's a tiny reference number on the label of the one key, and we were able to make out two digits, which was enough for us to confirm this."

"Where the safe is? You mean, you know exactly where this particular safe is located?" May now felt dizzy at the prospect.

"I'm ninety percent sure, yes. Come into the shop tomorrow, and I'll explain to you, and show you where it's located."

"Thank you, Pete. Thank you so much. I'll be there." May cut the call, feeling a sense of total disbelief.

The safe - the exact safe that these keys opened - existed. It was real and it had a location. May strongly believed that this safe would hold something, some information, on her sister.

And tomorrow, she would learn where it was.

NEVER LOOK BACK
(A May Moore Suspense Thriller—Book 7)

From #1 bestselling mystery and suspense author Blake Pierce comes a gripping new series: May Moore, 29, an average Midwestern woman and deputy sheriff, has always lived in the shadow of her older, brilliant FBI agent sister. Yet the sisters are united by the cold case of their missing younger sister—and when a new serial killer strikes in May's quiet, Minnesota lakeside town, it is May's turn to prove herself, to try to outshine her sister and the FBI, and, in this action-packed thriller, to outwit and hunt down a diabolical killer before he strikes again.

"A masterpiece of thriller and mystery."
—Books and Movie Reviews, Roberto Mattos (re Once Gone)

When victims of a new killer turn up on the farms outside town, attacked by an unusual murder weapon—a scythe—May must rush to decode the meaning—and to stop the killer before he strikes again.

As May begins to unearth stories of violence and secrets, she is drawn into an isolated and eerie world. Can she track down this killer before it's too late?

A page-turning and harrowing crime thriller featuring a brilliant and tortured Deputy Sheriff, the MAY MOORE series is a riveting mystery, packed with non-stop action, suspense, jaw-dropping twists, and driven by a breakneck pace that will keep you flipping pages late into the night.

Books #8 and #9 in the series—NEVER FORGET and NEVER LET GO—are also available!

"An edge of your seat thriller in a new series that keeps you turning pages! ...So many twists, turns and red herrings... I can't wait to see what happens next."
—Reader review (Her Last Wish)

"A strong, complex story about two FBI agents trying to stop a serial killer. If you want an author to capture your attention and have you guessing, yet trying to put the pieces together, Pierce is your author!"
—Reader review (Her Last Wish)

"A typical Blake Pierce twisting, turning, roller coaster ride suspense thriller. Will have you turning the pages to the last sentence of the last chapter!!!"
—Reader review (City of Prey)

"Right from the start we have an unusual protagonist that I haven't seen done in this genre before. The action is nonstop… A very atmospheric novel that will keep you turning pages well into the wee hours."
—Reader review (City of Prey)

"Everything that I look for in a book… a great plot, interesting characters, and grabs your interest right away. The book moves along at a breakneck pace and stays that way until the end. Now on go I to book two!"
—Reader review (Girl, Alone)

"Exciting, heart pounding, edge of your seat book… a must read for mystery and suspense readers!"
—Reader review (Girl, Alone)

BOOKS BY BLAKE PIERCE

NICKY LYONS MYSTERY SERIES
ALL MINE (Book #1)
ALL HIS (Book #2)
ALL HE SEES (Book #3)

CORA SHIELDS MYSTERY SERIES
UNDONE (Book #1)
UNWANTED (Book #2)
UNHINGED (Book #3)

MAY MOORE SUSPENSE THRILLER
NEVER RUN (Book #1)
NEVER TELL (Book #2)
NEVER LIVE (Book #3)
NEVER HIDE (Book #4)
NEVER FORGIVE (Book #5)
NEVER AGAIN (Book #6)

PAIGE KING MYSTERY SERIES
THE GIRL HE PINED (Book #1)
THE GIRL HE CHOSE (Book #2)
THE GIRL HE TOOK (Book #3)
THE GIRL HE WISHED (Book #4)
THE GIRL HE CROWNED (Book #5)
THE GIRL HE WATCHED (Book #6)

VALERIE LAW MYSTERY SERIES
NO MERCY (Book #1)
NO PITY (Book #2)
NO FEAR (Book #3)
NO SLEEP (Book #4)
NO QUARTER (Book #5)
NO CHANCE (Book #6)
NO REFUGE (Book #7)
NO GRACE (Book #8)

NO ESCAPE (Book #9)

RACHEL GIFT MYSTERY SERIES
HER LAST WISH (Book #1)
HER LAST CHANCE (Book #2)
HER LAST HOPE (Book #3)
HER LAST FEAR (Book #4)
HER LAST CHOICE (Book #5)
HER LAST BREATH (Book #6)
HER LAST MISTAKE (Book #7)
HER LAST DESIRE (Book #8)

AVA GOLD MYSTERY SERIES
CITY OF PREY (Book #1)
CITY OF FEAR (Book #2)
CITY OF BONES (Book #3)
CITY OF GHOSTS (Book #4)
CITY OF DEATH (Book #5)
CITY OF VICE (Book #6)

A YEAR IN EUROPE
A MURDER IN PARIS (Book #1)
DEATH IN FLORENCE (Book #2)
VENGEANCE IN VIENNA (Book #3)
A FATALITY IN SPAIN (Book #4)

ELLA DARK FBI SUSPENSE THRILLER
GIRL, ALONE (Book #1)
GIRL, TAKEN (Book #2)
GIRL, HUNTED (Book #3)
GIRL, SILENCED (Book #4)
GIRL, VANISHED (Book 5)
GIRL ERASED (Book #6)
GIRL, FORSAKEN (Book #7)
GIRL, TRAPPED (Book #8)
GIRL, EXPENDABLE (Book #9)
GIRL, ESCAPED (Book #10)
GIRL, HIS (Book #11)

LAURA FROST FBI SUSPENSE THRILLER

ALREADY GONE (Book #1)
ALREADY SEEN (Book #2)
ALREADY TRAPPED (Book #3)
ALREADY MISSING (Book #4)
ALREADY DEAD (Book #5)
ALREADY TAKEN (Book #6)
ALREADY CHOSEN (Book #7)
ALREADY LOST (Book #8)
ALREADY HIS (Book #9)

EUROPEAN VOYAGE COZY MYSTERY SERIES
MURDER (AND BAKLAVA) (Book #1)
DEATH (AND APPLE STRUDEL) (Book #2)
CRIME (AND LAGER) (Book #3)
MISFORTUNE (AND GOUDA) (Book #4)
CALAMITY (AND A DANISH) (Book #5)
MAYHEM (AND HERRING) (Book #6)

ADELE SHARP MYSTERY SERIES
LEFT TO DIE (Book #1)
LEFT TO RUN (Book #2)
LEFT TO HIDE (Book #3)
LEFT TO KILL (Book #4)
LEFT TO MURDER (Book #5)
LEFT TO ENVY (Book #6)
LEFT TO LAPSE (Book #7)
LEFT TO VANISH (Book #8)
LEFT TO HUNT (Book #9)
LEFT TO FEAR (Book #10)
LEFT TO PREY (Book #11)
LEFT TO LURE (Book #12)
LEFT TO CRAVE (Book #13)
LEFT TO LOATHE (Book #14)
LEFT TO HARM (Book #15)
LEFT TO RUIN (Book #16)

THE AU PAIR SERIES
ALMOST GONE (Book#1)
ALMOST LOST (Book #2)
ALMOST DEAD (Book #3)

ZOE PRIME MYSTERY SERIES
FACE OF DEATH (Book#1)
FACE OF MURDER (Book #2)
FACE OF FEAR (Book #3)
FACE OF MADNESS (Book #4)
FACE OF FURY (Book #5)
FACE OF DARKNESS (Book #6)

A JESSIE HUNT PSYCHOLOGICAL SUSPENSE SERIES
THE PERFECT WIFE (Book #1)
THE PERFECT BLOCK (Book #2)
THE PERFECT HOUSE (Book #3)
THE PERFECT SMILE (Book #4)
THE PERFECT LIE (Book #5)
THE PERFECT LOOK (Book #6)
THE PERFECT AFFAIR (Book #7)
THE PERFECT ALIBI (Book #8)
THE PERFECT NEIGHBOR (Book #9)
THE PERFECT DISGUISE (Book #10)
THE PERFECT SECRET (Book #11)
THE PERFECT FAÇADE (Book #12)
THE PERFECT IMPRESSION (Book #13)
THE PERFECT DECEIT (Book #14)
THE PERFECT MISTRESS (Book #15)
THE PERFECT IMAGE (Book #16)
THE PERFECT VEIL (Book #17)
THE PERFECT INDISCRETION (Book #18)
THE PERFECT RUMOR (Book #19)
THE PERFECT COUPLE (Book #20)
THE PERFECT MURDER (Book #21)
THE PERFECT HUSBAND (Book #22)
THE PERFECT SCANDAL (Book #23)
THE PERFECT MASK (Book #24)

CHLOE FINE PSYCHOLOGICAL SUSPENSE SERIES
NEXT DOOR (Book #1)
A NEIGHBOR'S LIE (Book #2)
CUL DE SAC (Book #3)

SILENT NEIGHBOR (Book #4)
HOMECOMING (Book #5)
TINTED WINDOWS (Book #6)

KATE WISE MYSTERY SERIES
IF SHE KNEW (Book #1)
IF SHE SAW (Book #2)
IF SHE RAN (Book #3)
IF SHE HID (Book #4)
IF SHE FLED (Book #5)
IF SHE FEARED (Book #6)
IF SHE HEARD (Book #7)

THE MAKING OF RILEY PAIGE SERIES
WATCHING (Book #1)
WAITING (Book #2)
LURING (Book #3)
TAKING (Book #4)
STALKING (Book #5)
KILLING (Book #6)

RILEY PAIGE MYSTERY SERIES
ONCE GONE (Book #1)
ONCE TAKEN (Book #2)
ONCE CRAVED (Book #3)
ONCE LURED (Book #4)
ONCE HUNTED (Book #5)
ONCE PINED (Book #6)
ONCE FORSAKEN (Book #7)
ONCE COLD (Book #8)
ONCE STALKED (Book #9)
ONCE LOST (Book #10)
ONCE BURIED (Book #11)
ONCE BOUND (Book #12)
ONCE TRAPPED (Book #13)
ONCE DORMANT (Book #14)
ONCE SHUNNED (Book #15)
ONCE MISSED (Book #16)
ONCE CHOSEN (Book #17)

MACKENZIE WHITE MYSTERY SERIES
BEFORE HE KILLS (Book #1)
BEFORE HE SEES (Book #2)
BEFORE HE COVETS (Book #3)
BEFORE HE TAKES (Book #4)
BEFORE HE NEEDS (Book #5)
BEFORE HE FEELS (Book #6)
BEFORE HE SINS (Book #7)
BEFORE HE HUNTS (Book #8)
BEFORE HE PREYS (Book #9)
BEFORE HE LONGS (Book #10)
BEFORE HE LAPSES (Book #11)
BEFORE HE ENVIES (Book #12)
BEFORE HE STALKS (Book #13)
BEFORE HE HARMS (Book #14)

AVERY BLACK MYSTERY SERIES
CAUSE TO KILL (Book #1)
CAUSE TO RUN (Book #2)
CAUSE TO HIDE (Book #3)
CAUSE TO FEAR (Book #4)
CAUSE TO SAVE (Book #5)
CAUSE TO DREAD (Book #6)

KERI LOCKE MYSTERY SERIES
A TRACE OF DEATH (Book #1)
A TRACE OF MURDER (Book #2)
A TRACE OF VICE (Book #3)
A TRACE OF CRIME (Book #4)
A TRACE OF HOPE (Book #5)

www.ingramcontent.com/pod-product-compliance
Lightning Source LLC
Chambersburg PA
CBHW032009120726
47902CB00014B/2029